PRAISE FOR

The End of the Wild

A New York Public Library Best Books for Kids Pick

A *Kirkus* Best Middle-Grade Books Pick

A *New York Times* Book Review Editors' Choice

A Parents' Choice Award Winner

★ "This nuanced take on a pressing issue is an important one. Middle-grade readers will find much to think about in this **beautifully written** story."
—*Kirkus Reviews*, starred review

★ "Helget **confronts substantial subjects** like poverty, environmentalism, and mental illness, **injecting humor and hope** to provide balance. Without lecturing, she **encourages readers to be thoughtful and curious.**"
—*Publishers Weekly*, starred review

★ "Helget has penned **a rich narrative**, laced with astute observations on poverty, grief, forgiveness, and environmental concerns....An uncommonly fine account of perseverance and understanding in the face of adversity." —*Booklist*, starred review

The End of the Wild

NICOLE HELGET

LB

LITTLE, BROWN AND COMPANY
New York   Boston

Text copyright © 2017 by Nicole Helget
Illustrations copyright © 2017 by Oamul Lu
Text in excerpt from *Wonder at the Edge of the World* copyright © 2015 by Nicole Helget
Illustrations in excerpt from *Wonder at the Edge of the World* copyright © 2015 by Marcos Calo

Cover illustration copyright © 2018 by R Kikuo Johnson. Cover design by Marcie Lawrence.
Cover copyright © 2018 by Hachette Book Group, Inc.

Little, Brown and Company
Hachette Book Group
1290 Avenue of the Americas, New York, NY 10104
Visit us at LBYR.com

Originally published in hardcover and ebook by Little, Brown and Company in April 2017
First Trade Paperback Edition: June 2018

Little, Brown and Company is a division of Hachette Book Group, Inc. The Little, Brown name and logo are trademarks of Hachette Book Group, Inc.

The publisher is not responsible for websites (or their content) that are not owned by the publisher.

The Library of Congress has cataloged the hardcover edition as follows:
Names: Helget, Nicole Lea, 1976– author.
Title: The end of the wild / Nicole Helget.
Description: First edition. | New York ; Boston : Little, Brown and Company, 2017.
| Summary: "Eleven-year-old Fern helps to take care of her impoverished family by foraging for food in the forest, but when a fracking company rolls into town, she realizes that her peaceful woods and her family's livelihood could be threatened"— Provided by publisher.
Identifiers: LCCN 2016031990| ISBN 9780316245111 (hardback) | ISBN 9780316245128 (ebook) | ISBN 9780316364966 (library edition ebook)
Subjects: | CYAC: Family life—Fiction. | Stepfathers—Fiction. | Forests and forestry—Fiction. | Poverty—Fiction. | Schools—Fiction. | Science projects—Fiction. | Environmental protection—Fiction. | Social action—Fiction. | BISAC: JUVENILE FICTION / Social Issues / Homelessness & Poverty. | JUVENILE FICTION / Nature & the Natural World / Environment. | JUVENILE FICTION / Family / Alternative Family. | JUVENILE FICTION / Cooking & Food. | JUVENILE FICTION / Social Issues / Self-Esteem & Self-Reliance. | JUVENILE FICTION / Animals / Dogs. | JUVENILE FICTION / Lifestyles / Country Life. | JUVENILE FICTION / Social Issues / Death & Dying.
Classification: LCC PZ7.H374085 End 2017 | DDC [Fic]—dc23
LC record available at https://lccn.loc.gov/2016031990

ISBNs: 978-0-316-24513-5 (pbk.), 978-0-316-24512-8 (ebook)

Printed in the United States of America

LSC-C

10 9 8 7 6 5 4 3 2 1

*To Softy, Spirit, Snuffy, Pierps, Pony,
and Polar Bear, good dogs past
and present*

Chapter 1

A hint of winter is on the morning wind. Waist-long, walnut-colored hair slaps my face. A gray tendril grows from just behind one ear. I don't know why I have gray hairs at eleven years old. I just do. My eyes are gray, too. Steel, actually, is what Toivo, my stepdad, says. Like what my nerves are made of, he says. If you ask me, my eyes are way too big, like an alien's.

A wild pack of family dogs yaps along Millner's property fence. One's got black ears pointed upward. Another dog, short and squat, has brown ears down long. He keeps his nose high, so his ears don't drag on the ground.

One dog has nubs where his ears should be. And another, a mottled terrier that licks his nether regions, has one ear northwest and one ear southeast. An ugly pup, spotty and short-furred, has a wood tick the size of a dime attached to the side of his eye. A few regular-sized canines of other dog colors scratch their ears and bite away chunks of mud from between their toes. They bark at me and make a tetchy racket.

Ruff! Grrr! Yip! Oww-wow-wow!

In total, they're a gang of eight or nine canines belonging to our neighbor, Horace Millner, who is a killer.

I call one of them Ranger. He's a yellow-and-brown German shepherd. The fur around his muzzle is silver with age. He stares at me as though he is full of big thoughts. Ranger has a way about him that is different from the other dogs. It is a way about him that I like. He's a no-nonsense kind of dog. He's wily and smart and courageous. There are just some things you can tell about animals by watching them as long as I've watched these ones.

I pat my hand on my thigh. "Here, boy," I say. "Here, Ranger." Ranger cocks his head sideways. I'd like to have Ranger for myself. Millner doesn't deserve such a fine animal.

Ranger turns and pretends to ignore me. He steps his front paws up and down a little bit as though he's considering it, jumping the fence and running to me.

I inch my boot forward toward the fence and slowly raise my hand out in front of me.

Ranger turns his ears to me and puts his nose up, but he doesn't spook off. My boot scratches along the gravel road again. Ranger's tail lifts up.

"It's okay," I coax. "I'm not going to hurt you. It's okay."

The other dogs glance back and forth between Ranger and me as I creep forward.

"That's a good dog," I say. When I'm within touching distance, the fur on the back of Ranger's neck stands up. One of the other dogs growls low, so low that even though I can barely hear it, my neck vibrates.

Ranger snaps at that dog.

I jump back.

"Okay," I say. "Okay." I back away from the pack.

One last time, I lean over and pat my thigh. "Here, boy," I say.

He doesn't come, though. He must feel some loyalty to the rest of those wretched animals.

"Suit yourself," I say, and I turn away. No one is

awake yet out here in the country. We live about a mile outside Colter, a small Michigan town, which has got a school, a community college, a beauty parlor, two churches, one cemetery, a few bars, Grandpa's pipe factory, a couple of auto garages, and not much else except a lot of nosy people.

This morning, the sunrise cuts like glass shards across the emptied cornfield, spills over the gravel road, and spears into the grove. The brown-and-orange leaf canopy shivers with the wind. Oak trees hold on to their leaves in autumn even as the rest of the trees lose theirs. I spy an oak with full branches. This time of year, middle of October, hen-of-the-woods mushrooms grow in layered bunches at the base of oaks. They are bark-colored—tan, brown, and gray—and have leaf-shaped petals.

From my back pocket, I pull a canvas bag and drape it over my shoulders like a shawl. I wish I had grabbed my jacket, even if it was already too small last fall. I need a new one, but I hate to bring it up with Toivo. We're always broke or "cash strapped," as Toivo says. That just means we have no money.

At the base of the oak tree, I stop. A hen-of-the-woods grows near the gnarled roots. With my pocketknife, I slice the mushroom from its stem and slip it into the bag. Hen-of-the-woods are very good eating, if you ask me. They taste like turkey or chicken, I guess. They even chew up in a birdy respect.

A bright stick of white pokes out from some leaves. After brushing the leaves aside, I find a bone. The leg bone of a deer, looks like to me.

I take that, too.

On my walk back home, I pass where the dogs were. I set the bone near the fence. I have a hunch Ranger will know it's from me.

By the time I'm halfway home, the sun is a big egg yolk. The air out here swipes like long cat nails at my face, but I just smile. Out here, my stomach isn't knotted about being hungry. My fingers don't tingle in panic over having no money. My breath isn't clipped short over minding my unruly brothers. My head doesn't burn with worry over my undone homework.

Soft, quick footsteps pad behind me. I stop and perk my ears.

The footsteps stop, too.

I check the road and the ditch and the edges of the field and the grove. Though I don't see anyone or anything, I hear someone or something breathing wetly.

The worst thing you can do when a predator has you in its sights is stand still with a hard-beating heart and a trembling upper lip. The worst, worst thing you can do is start sweating out a scared odor.

If I owned a dog like Ranger, he'd be here beside me right now, ready to attack whoever or whatever is out there waiting to kill me.

I walk again, with my fist clenched. I scan the ground for a weapon-suited stone or stick. After a few paces, footsteps rustle behind me again. I reach down and take up a forked branch, perfect for jabbing two eyes with one stab. I spin with my weapon raised.

But, again, no one's there.

Except my intuition tells me someone or something *is*.

"Where are you?" I demand. "Come out!" Maybe it's a bear. We get them around here sometimes. Or maybe it's Horace Millner. Maybe he's crouching in the ditch weeds. Maybe he's mad at me for being in his woods. Or maybe he'd like to get rid of me, since I'm a constant reminder of his crime.

"Who's there?" I say. To be tricky, I walk backward just to see if whoever is following me will listen for my footsteps before showing himself. A couple of steps back, I do see something walking toward me on the road. The angle of the piercing light makes it impossible to identify.

My heart throbs like a frog's throat. I walk backward a bit quicker until I nearly fall down. The footsteps pick up speed. I raise my stick.

Don't panic, I tell myself. *Don't faint. Don't run. Stand your ground. That's what buffalo do.*

Run! That's what deer do.

I turn and dart. My arms slice the air, and my feet beat the ground. Even so, the footsteps gain on me. Up ahead, I'm surprised to see a bulldozer that reads KLOCHE'S HYDRAULIC FRACTURING parked on the side of the road. I dash for it, grab hold of the fender, and lift myself up into the cab. I collapse on the seat. The engine is warm, which means it's only recently been running.

For a few seconds, I squeeze my eyes closed and wait for a bear to bite down on my head or a knife to stab my back or a rope to get looped around my neck.

But nothing happens. Finally, I straighten up and push the hair behind my ears. I turn and look.

Woof!

I squint and put my hand above my eyes like a visor.

Woof! Woof!

Ranger sits in the middle of the road. His wagging tail sweeps gravel back and forth. At his forepaws sits the leg bone I left him.

Woof, he barks again.

Then a high whistle pierces the morning air. Ranger's ears go up. He picks up his bone, circles around, and strolls back toward the fence.

On the other side of it, Horace Millner the killer stands staring at me with his arms crossed.

I gasp. Because the sun is behind him, to me he looks like a dark, scary shadow. Was he watching me pick mushrooms from his woods? Did he see me try to coax his dog away?

For a while, all I can do is steady my air and gape at him until he turns around and disappears like a ghost into the woods.

Ranger trots after him with the big bone hanging off one side of his mouth. When I can't see them anymore, I shout, "You're welcome, Ranger!"

Chapter 2

I throw my backpack—Toivo's old marine rucksack—under my desk and dive into my chair. The classroom clock says it's 7:59.

Alkomso, who sits behind me, kicks my chair. "You were nearly late *again*," she whispers. Alkomso Isak has been my best friend since third grade.

"I had to get my brothers to their classrooms," I say. "Anyway, I beat Mr. Flores, and that's all that matters."

"How's your STEM project going?" she says.

"Don't even ask." Just then, the bell rings. Mr. Flores, our science teacher, slides into the classroom.

"Juuuuust under the wire," he says. He's only about

twenty-five years old, but he's already wrinkly around the eyes. Mr. Flores's face is pale, like the underside of a mushroom. He's wearing jeans and flip-flops and an old T-shirt with a big picture of Dolly Parton on it. He's holding a big cardboard box. "Are we ready to study some bird specimens today?"

Some kids groan, and some kids hoot and holler.

Mr. Flores opens the box and begins pulling out stuffed birds—a pheasant that looks about to take flight and a mallard sitting on a nest.

"Ew," says Margot Peterson. "Those are disgusting. I am not touching those."

"No worries, Margot," says Mr. Flores. "You don't have to touch them if you don't want to."

Mr. Flores usually makes science fun. Lots of times, he takes our class outside to study spiderwebs, compare rock compositions, identify clouds, observe tadpoles, and classify leaves. In the classroom, he sets up tons of experiments and plays videos about climate change and animal testing and the origin of the earth.

Mark-Richard Haala, who is in serious need of a new pair of sneakers because his smell like raisins, raises his hand. "Mr. Flores? I have a major problem with my STEM project."

The Science, Technology, Engineering, and Math fair is in a couple of weeks, and I don't even have a topic yet. Just the mention of it sets my stomach on the spin cycle.

"Why can't we just call it a science fair, like people used to?" asks Alkomso. "Why do we have to call it STEM now?"

Mr. Flores shrugs, then pulls out a glass case with what looks like a pink pigeon inside and places it delicately on the top of his desk. "What's your problem, Mark-Richard?" he asks.

"I have to change my topic. All the plants for my project already died."

"All of them?" asks Mr. Flores. He sits on top of his desk, lifts a white owl out of the box, and sets it on his lap.

"Yeah," says Mark-Richard. "Now my hypothesis is ruined."

Mr. Flores straightens some of the feathers on the owl. "Sorry about your plants. But just because your data doesn't support your hypothesis doesn't mean that your project wasn't successful."

Mark-Richard slumps in his seat. His long bangs hang over his eyes. "Yeah, but even my control plants in the good soil are, like, all droopy and hanging down. And the ones I planted in sand are brown and crunchy."

Margot scoffs. "Duh, Marky," she says. "That's because your parents smoke in the house all the time. And you probably forgot to water them."

Margot's friends giggle with her.

I spin around and look at Alkomso, who looks at me like *Can you believe her?*

Mark-Richard straightens up and scowls at Margot. "I *did* water them. But they got these little tiny bugs all over them." He wipes his nose with the back of his sleeve. "The bugs made webby things on the leaves, and they all turned brown."

Mr. Flores lights up. "Now, see? That's fascinating. Your project was a success even if it didn't produce the result you intended." He sets the owl next to the glass box and pulls out a small plastic bag of bones.

"It was?"

"Of course," says Mr. Flores. "What effect do aphids, or whatever kind of bugs they are, have on plants?"

"Death," says Mark-Richard. The whole class laughs.

Mr. Flores chuckles, too. "Yes. They kill them. But

how? And why did the variable plants become infested faster?"

Mark-Richard flips his hair out of his eyes. "I don't know."

"True learning comes from being open to wrong answers," says Mr. Flores.

Margot sniffs. "Well, I'm going to make sure my conclusion matches my hypothesis. I want to get that purple ribbon."

Mr. Flores shakes his head. "Margot, Margot, Margot. There's more to life than ribbons."

"Whatever, Mr. Flores," Margot says. "You're not the one judging the fair. My mom says that the projects that win every year are the ones with really nice-looking poster boards." Margot's mom is on the school board. "And the winner gets two hundred and fifty dollars."

"Two hundred and fifty dollars!" I shout. I clap my hand over my mouth. I don't usually say anything, much less blurt it out to the whole class.

I can feel the eyes of all my classmates on me. I scooch down lower in my chair.

"Yes," Margot says, and drums her fingers on her desk. "I need to win that money."

How could Margot say that? Her parents are probably the wealthiest people in Colter. I'm the one who needs to win that money. Maybe I could pay the propane bill so we wouldn't have to chop so much wood from the grove to heat our house.

Alkomso twists around in her seat to look at Margot. "As if you even need the money, Margot. You can just ask your dad for whatever you want."

Mark-Richard wipes his nose with his sleeve again. "If I won two hundred and fifty dollars, I'd buy my brother and me new bikes."

Margot takes a lip gloss out of her pocket. "For your information, Alkomso, I *do* need the money." She smears the pink gloss over her bottom lip. "For a new phone." She slides an iPhone off to the corner of her desk. "This one's a piece of junk."

"I'll take that piece of junk," says Mark-Richard.

"All right," says Mr. Flores. "Settle down. And, Margot, put the phone away. No phones in class."

The sound of Mr. Flores's voice is drowned out as a big truck rumbles past, rattling the windows of the classroom. Mr. Flores looks out and grimaces.

"What is it?" Alkomso asks.

Mr. Flores stares and doesn't answer. Some of us

stand up to see what Mr. Flores is looking at. Soon a semitruck with a bed full of long white pipes whizzes by. I can just make out the word KLOCHE'S on the door.

"Hey," I say. "I saw a bulldozer with that same name on it this morning."

Mr. Flores's head snaps around. "Where?"

"On the side of the gravel road, near Millner's woods."

Mr. Flores groans, then sighs. "We'd better start our lesson. Everyone, back in your seats."

Alkomso and I look at each other and shrug. Mr. Flores starts talking about hollow bird bones and pectoral muscles and feathers with vanes and barbs and bird flight. But every time the windows rattle, he loses his place in his demonstration. Finally, he tells us to open our textbooks and read to ourselves.

"Mr. Flores," I say, "is there something wrong?"

His cheeks blossom into two red dots, and his eyes squint. If Mr. Flores has an angry face, this is what it looks like. "I'm pretty sure there is," he says.

"With the woods?" I ask.

"Well…" he begins. He rubs his chin and blinks a couple of times, as if wondering if he should continue.

"Are the woods in trouble? I practically live in those

woods," I say. I think about all the food I find for my family there.

"You and lots of animals," he says. "Millner's woods is an important ecosystem." He rubs his chin again and mumbles something.

"What?" I ask.

He clears his throat. "Wherever Kloche's goes, disaster follows."

I'm too stunned to respond. Kids murmur to each other. Someone says, "What do you mean?"

Mr. Flores tells us to get back to work. He sits behind his desk and opens up his laptop. He clacks his fingers against the keys and peers at the screen.

Mark-Richard and I scoot our desks next to Alkomso's. She flips her textbook to the chapter on bird flight. "What's up with Mr. Flores?" she whispers.

"It's those trucks," says Mark-Richard. "And that company. Whatever they're about, Mr. Flores doesn't like it."

"Maybe the Three Misfit-keteers could keep it down?" Margot says.

The class giggles. One of Margot's friends slaps her desk and repeats, *"Three Misfit-keteers!"*

"Shut up, Margot," says Alkomso. "You're just jealous

that Fern is prettier than you even though you paint your whole entire face with blush and eye shadow."

Margot's thinly plucked eyebrows squish together.

My cheeks burn red. "Alkomso!" I hiss. "Don't say that."

"Well, it's true," she says. "Margot thinks she's all that, and I'm sick of it."

"Hey!" Mr. Flores shouts. "Knock it off and put your noses back in your books."

Margot scratches out words in big letters on her notebook. When she's done, she shows us. *Fern's clothes are hideous*, it says. *And at least I don't have gray hair.*

Mark-Richard sniffles and wipes his nose. "Don't listen to her," he whispers to me.

"Guys," I whisper, "let's just read this chapter."

But Alkomso can't hold back. "Margot," she says, loud enough for the entire class to hear, "your hair is going to fall out from all that poison you put in it."

"At least everyone knows I have hair," says Margot. "At least I'm not covering mine up all the time."

Alkomso straightens her hijab. Her cheeks puff up like she's about to let Margot have it.

Mr. Flores stands up and shouts, "That's *it*!

Consider this your official warning for a quiz tomorrow on the bird-flight chapter."

The bell rings. Everyone stands up and gathers their things.

"Thanks a lot, Alkomso," says Margot. "You got us all in trouble."

"Whatever, Margot," Alkomso says.

As I walk past Mr. Flores, I say, "Sorry about that."

He sighs. "It's all right." I look past his shoulder to his computer screen, which is opened to a page that says *Kloche's Hydraulic Fracturing: Powering Tomorrow's Future*. A map at the bottom of the screen shows Colter, with a big red dot a few miles away from my house and a smaller red dot near Millner's woods.

"Hey," I say. "What's that red dot?"

"Fracking site," he says. "How can I help you, Fern?"

I stare at the computer screen. "Um—you see—I, uh—" I stammer.

Mr. Flores smiles. "Let me guess. You haven't started your STEM project."

I smile, too, even though I'm embarrassed. "I'm just not sure what to do it on."

He nods. "Think about what really interests you,

Fern. Think about your passions. Think about what you care about."

"Can't you just give me some ideas?" I ask.

"I could," he says.

I sigh in relief.

"But I'm not going to." He leans forward. "Fern, you live and breathe science every day. I know where you live. Science is all around you in the soil, the trees, the weather, the animals, the way you heat your home, the way you put food on the table." He sits back in his chair. "Rise to the occasion," he says. "I know you can."

Deep down, I know he's right. But that doesn't put me any closer to an idea. "Thanks." I turn and begin to head to my next class when another truck rumbles past and shakes the window glass.

"Mr. Flores," I say. "What exactly *is* fracking?"

"Drilling."

"Like, for oil?" I ask.

"Sort of," he says. "Natural gas. Miles and miles and miles beneath the surface."

"The smaller dot on the map," I say. "That's near where I live."

"Yeah," he says. "Looks like that's where the wastewater pond is going to go," he says.

"What's a waste—"

The bell rings. "You're late," he says. "You'd better get to your next class, Fern."

"Yeah, but—" I start.

I take one last glance at the screen. It looks like someone smashed a bloody wood tick right over my woods.

Chapter 3

After the last bell, I collect my little brothers, Mikko and Alexi, from their classrooms, and Alkomso and Mark-Richard do the same. We walk through Colter and on home together. On the outskirts of Colter is where Alkomso and her family live in an apartment. Mark-Richard and his brother, Gary, live in a trailer out near us. They're close enough that sometimes we can even hear their parents arguing and throwing stuff.

"What are you doing for your STEM project?" Mark-Richard asks Alkomso and me.

"Don't even mention it," I say. "I haven't started."

"Me, either," says Alkomso. "But that prize sure

sounds sweet. What would you buy with two hundred and fifty dollars? Do you think they give it to you in cash? I've never even seen a hundred-dollar bill in real life."

"Bikes, for sure," says Mark-Richard. "And a whole bunch of corn dogs."

What's weird right now is that I can't think of what I'd spend two hundred and fifty dollars on. Even though all the things I don't have bother me all the time, I've gotten used to being bothered in that way.

Alkomso grips the sleeve of my coat, Toivo's old wool shirt. "Maybe you could get yourself a new jacket?"

"Yeah," I say. "Maybe a new coat."

"I'd take my whole family out for cheese pizza." As we approach her apartment building, Alkomso's little brothers nearly dash out into the street before she grabs each of them and pulls them back onto the sidewalk.

"No!" she says. "Don't you ever cross the street without me."

They protest and say they're big enough, but Alkomso gives them a face like she means it, and they stop. A truck goes roaring by. "See?" she says. "You could get hit!"

The back of the truck has a bed full of pipes.

"Aren't those the pipes your grandpa's factory makes?" Mark-Richard asks me. Sometimes Mark-Richard's dad works for Grandpa's factory. Lots of people in town do, since there aren't very many other places to get a job. But they get hired and laid off, so their jobs aren't real reliable.

"I guess so." Grandpa doesn't always treat his workers that great, and since a lot of his workers' kids are my classmates, I hear about it when their moms and dads are unemployed because of Grandpa. "I don't care about that stupid factory."

"I would if I were you," says Alkomso. "Maybe you'll inherit it someday!"

"I wonder where the trucks are going," says Mark-Richard. His dad also sometimes works as a truck driver, which is another pretty common way to try and make a living around here. "That gravel road is too small for that kind of traffic, and it just leads out into the country."

I think about the map on Mr. Flores's screen. I think about drilling. *Miles and miles beneath the surface*, Mr. Flores had said. *Wastewater pond.* I shudder.

Alkomso takes her brothers by the hand and calls,

"See you!" over her shoulder as they cross the road to go home.

Mark-Richard and I continue on. The sidewalk ends, and the road turns to dirt right where the Colter water tower stands. On one side of the road are farm fields, and on the other are woods. When a car comes, we move off to the woods side.

Mark-Richard grabs my arm and pulls me aside.

"Hey!" I say.

He points to the ground, where there's a big brown mound.

My brothers run over.

"Bear poop!" Mikko shouts.

"Get a stick!" Alexi says.

"Don't you dare," I say. "You are not playing with bear poop."

Gary puts the toe of his boot right to the edge of it. Mark-Richard yanks him away. "Don't mess your shoes. Those are the only ones you have."

The boys whine, but they listen and move on down the road.

"You don't like your grandpa much, do you?" Mark-Richard sneezes into his elbow.

"You got a cold again?" I ask.

"All the time," he says. "You don't have to answer about your grandpa. I was just curious."

"It's okay. Grandpa thinks he knows what's best for everyone without asking them."

"Yeah, I understand. But think about all the cool stuff you could have if you lived with him."

"I don't ever want to live with him," I say. "I want to stay with Toivo."

Mark-Richard's parents don't take care of their kids half as good as Toivo takes care of us. They don't act very grown up. Last year, Mark-Richard's baby sister got taken away and put into foster care in a home four hours away. Now he only gets to see her once a month. When she first got removed, Mark-Richard cried in school for about a month straight.

We keep walking until there's a little clearing in the woods, where Mark-Richard's trailer is. A couple of overweight cats play with a pop can. A few cords of wood are stacked up messily along the driveway. Mark-Richard's house is heated with a wood stove in winter, like ours.

"You'll need a lot more wood than that," I say.

"I know it. Mom says Dad's a lazy son of a gun for not cutting more. But I know where a dead tree finally fell down, so I'll go out and hack off the easy branches. Come on, Gary."

Gary clings to Mikko. "I don't want to go home. I want to go to Mikko's house."

"Some other time." Mark-Richard puts his arm around Gary. "Maybe Mom made us a snack." He leads Gary up the driveway. "Bye," he says to me.

"Bye." I stare up at the trailer. Mark-Richard's mom stands at the screen door. I raise my hand and wave at her. She turns away. "Wanna walk to school together tomorrow?" I shout after Mark-Richard.

He gives me a thumbs-up.

When we get home from school, my little brothers race off into the woods. I find Toivo in the shed. He's got three wild turkeys spread-eagle on a butchering table, and a headless, gutted deer strung up from the rafters. The head and a gloopy pile of innards rest on a garbage bag. A bucket of water steams at his boots. His hands drip crimson with blood. Bits of fur and feathers stick to his fingers.

"What's a wastewater pond?" I ask.

He spins around. "Hello to you, too," he says. He

talks with a cigarette dangling out of the corner of his mouth. "Yes, I had a nice day, as well."

"Sorry," I say. "Hi. How was your day?"

"Fine, thanks," he says. He points to the corner of the garage, to where I left the bag with my mushroom in it this morning. "What did you find for us?"

"A big one," I say. I bring the sack over and open the top.

"Very nice!" He nods. "Want to pluck the turkey legs?" With his knife, he points to the water bucket. "Got the hot water right here."

Plucking feathers used to be Mom's job. Now it's mine, ever since Mom and Baby Matti were killed in a car crash right near the water tower on the edge of town.

In a couple of days, it'll be two years ago. It's a really sad story, but everybody has one, and lots of times somebody important in the tale is dead.

Toivo slides his knife around the joints of the turkey he's working on and splits the breastbone. Then he goes to the deer hanging from the rafter and slaps its side. "Look at this guy. I've seen him hanging around in the woods, and this morning I got a perfect shot off."

I happen to know that Toivo can't afford a hunting

license and has gotten in trouble before for poaching. Unlike most other hunters, though, he's doesn't do it for fun. He does it because we need the food. "He's huge," I say. "Lots of meat. Look at those back straps."

He reaches up and tugs tight on the rope's knot. Toivo is tall and reedy. He smokes cigarettes pretty regularly to keep his jitters tamped down. His time in the Iraq War made him jumpy. Sometimes he talks about his time in the marines, but most of the time he doesn't.

"Indeed," he says. "To be honest, I'm relieved. We were getting pretty low on supplies there."

I think about the biscuit-and-ketchup sandwiches the boys and I choked down for lunch and how nice it would have been to have had a slice or two of venison sausage on them.

I hold the turkey leg by the claw and dunk the muscle in hot water, lift it up and down, up and down, until the skin relaxes enough for me to rub the feathers off. Then I settle into an old, crooked chair and pull the feathers out by the handful, flap them off onto a plastic bag.

"Got homework?" Toivo asks.

"No," I lie.

"Better get it done after this," he says.

I'm not sure if he knows that I lied or if he didn't hear what I said. Toivo lost the hearing in one of his ears in the war. He wears a hearing aid to help, but it malfunctions all the time, and he says the VA won't buy him a new one.

"Well, I do have to come up with a STEM project," I say.

"Gotta keep the grades up," he adds. He pinches the cigarette from his lips and snuffs it out in an ashtray on the table. "I got another letter from Children's Protective Services today," he adds. "And your gramps left a message on the phone."

I tear ferociously at the turkey feathers. Gramps and Children's Protective Services are on Toivo's tail all the time. They think my brothers and I would be better off living with Gramps, with his big wallet, big house, big pool, big garage full of classic cars, and big bank account. They don't call Gramps "Big John" for nothing.

"I guess I'd better come up with something good, then." If I get an F, it'll just be more fodder for Grandpa to target Toivo.

If Mom were here, she'd have this sorted out in no time. Even though she taught English, Mom loved science. She was always reading plant books and physics books about multiple universes.

When I let myself dwell on Mom and Matti being gone, I can't breathe. My lungs feel as though they are the size of maple tree seeds. That my little brothers and I might be taken away from Toivo feels like an extra airlessness that makes me dizzy.

Technically, Toivo is not my dad. My father is long gone. I don't even know where he is and can't remember ever knowing him. I was a baby when he took off. Mom met Toivo at the school where she taught. After the war, he went there to take some classes. Even though she was ten years older than he was, he fell in love with her when he took a writing class from her.

Mom married Toivo when I was three. I was the flower girl. I don't remember much, but I've seen photos. I wore a green dress with a black sash. After the wedding, Toivo and Mom had Mikko, Alexi, and Matti. Toivo's the only father I've ever known. I don't know why he didn't adopt me while Mom was still alive. Maybe they just didn't imagine that there would ever be a day when they'd be separated, when Mom would be gone, when the law would get to decide what makes a family.

"I'm not going with them," I whisper. I stop pluck-ing and shake the sticky mess off my hands. Globs of feathers fly. One smacks Toivo right on the neck.

"Hey!" he says. He scrapes it off and plops it on the ground.

"Sorry," I say.

My grandfather never liked Toivo. To make his point, Grandpa cut Mom off from his money the day she and Toivo married. Since she's been gone, papers from Grandpa's lawyer, from the family service people, and from the courts clutter our mailbox practically every day.

They say that Toivo is a chain smoker.

That Toivo is unemployed.

That Toivo neglects our schoolwork.

That Toivo "fails to maintain a clean living environ-ment."

That Toivo "suffers from severe psychological distress."

That Toivo is an "unfit parent."

All those things are true except the last one. That last one isn't the least bit honest. If anyone would just ask me or ask my little brothers, they'd know. But no one asks us.

"They say I'm no good." Toivo sighs. I'm not sure if he heard what I said or if he's just talking. He shakes his head. "But I do my best."

He comes over and plops the next turkey leg right on my lap. "You're my girl," he says. "No matter what. Always have been, always will be." He gives my shoulder a squeeze and leaves a bloody handprint.

I dig my short fingernails into the loose, pale turkey skin and capture the final needle-y pinfeather, just a small black speck that can cause all kinds of problems if one gets stuck in your gums. I flick it to the ground.

I hold up the leg. "There," I say. "That one's all done. Ready for the frying pan."

"I do enjoy fried turkey skin," he says quietly. "Your mom could sure fry up a turkey leg." He turns and looks at me. Toivo's got hazel eyes, the color of a bullfrog. Matti had them, too. "Remember that?" he asks.

I remember. Butter, flour, onion, salt, hot pan. *Keep it simple*, she always told me about cooking.

Toivo chuckles to himself. "You know, when I met her, she'd couldn't cook a noodle."

I already know this story, but I don't mind hearing it again. "No way," I say. I dunk the second leg in the scalding water. "Mom was a great cook!"

Fried Wild Turkey Legs

Melt a stick of butter in a medium-hot fry pan. Dust four turkey legs (preferably from two separate birds—ha-ha!) with flour and fry them. Turn them over after a minute. Turn heat to low. Add two cans of beer, a whole onion, and a cup of morel mushrooms. Simmer for two hours. Eat them like a barbarian.

He shakes his head. "Nooooooo. Not at first," he says. "When I met her, you were living on take-out pizzas."

"What?"

"Yep," he says. "I never expected her to cook, you understand. I just couldn't eat that junk she was serving. Boxed macaroni and frozen corn dogs. Makes my insides work like a cement mixer. So I took over the cooking, and she caught on. She started that little recipe book you have."

That little recipe book is my prized possession. I keep it on my nightstand. It's a simple spiral notebook with extra pages shoved in it or paper-clipped to the back cover. Mom's handwriting loops and twists and turns into directions for rabbit stew, creamed pheasant, wild parsnip soup, crabapple cider, mulberry preserves, and everything else we eat and drink. By now, I know many of the recipes by heart. Still, I like to have the book open when I'm cooking. That way Mom feels right next to me.

My whole head gets hot, and I can practically feel my scalp frying behind my ear, turning more brown hairs gray.

Toivo and I work quietly for a while, cutting, trimming, plucking, and wrapping the meat in butcher's paper. I think about asking him where he poached the turkeys, if someone from the Department of Natural Resources saw him, or if he had any luck finding a job today. But I don't.

A crash from behind the shed breaks the silence. Toivo and I both jump.

"I'm gonna get you!" That's Mikko. His nose is always stuffed up.

Another crash.

"You are not, you ratface!" Alexi.

A thump.

"I'm gonna tell on you!"

A bump.

A scuffle.

"I'm gonna tell on you, you smelly idiot!"

Hard footsteps.

Boots scratching gravel.

Heavy breathing.

More sounds of scrapping.

"You're an ugly, stupid fartface!"

Running. A screen-door squeak. A door slam.

Toivo chuckles. "I guess your brothers are back from their adventures," he says to me.

My little brothers spend a lot of time in the woods,

poking sticks into mole holes, digging clams out of the stream, shaking hornet nests from tree limbs, and throwing deer-poop pellets at each other.

Toivo straightens his face, takes a deep breath, and roars, "You boys better knock that off!" His face wrinkles up with smiling. Then his face flattens and he says, "Did you ask me something about a wastewater pond earlier?"

"Nah," I say. "It's nothing."

He returns to his work of filling the freezer with meat before winter comes.

Chapter 4

Machinery rumbling past our house and toward the woods wakes me from a dream about Ranger. In the dream, the sky rolls with thunder. The ground shakes. I'm petting Ranger, but when I lift my hand, fur drifts off him and falls to the ground. When I look at the ground, the fur has turned into a bush of rose hips.

I lie on my pillow for a minute, thinking. Once the truck has passed, it's so quiet I can hear a mouse scratching behind the wall. I tap on the wall, and the mouse stops.

Then another roaring truck rattles the window,

shakes the quiet house. I sit up and press my nose to the windowpane. It's a Kloche's Hydraulic Fracturing truck with a trailer full of Grandpa's pipes. The tail-wind shocks loads of leaves off the trees. Even after the truck is out of sight, the leaves twizzle.

This morning, the air outside looks hazy in the sunrise. We live on a long dirt road. Usually, it's very quiet out here. I like it that way. Quiet and private.

Toivo likes it out here, too. He grew up in the woods. He comes from a long line of lumberjacks, true all the way back to Finland. His father was a logger for one of the mills that used to exist in this town. When Toivo was twelve, on the last week the mill was open before foreclosure shut it down, his father fell out of a tree and died. Once in a while, when I look at Toivo, my jaw gets tight when I think about that. He probably looks at me and gets the same chokehold on his throat.

Right behind the last, another truck cruises by. I wonder if trucks will always be blowing by now.

I throw the blanket off my legs. The jeans I was wearing yesterday, they're a bit stiff and smell a little like turkey feathers, but they'll do for another day, so I slip them on.

I grab Mom's recipe book and sneak out of my room.

Past the boys' bedroom, I tiptoe and avoid the creaky floorboards. Mikko and Alexi remain fast asleep, snoring, drooling, and draped over each other in the bed they share like a couple of bear cubs in a den.

In the kitchen, Toivo sits at the table, drinking coffee. He's opening envelopes and scribbling checks to bill collectors.

"Good morning," he whispers.

"Morning." I flip on the light switch for the basement.

"Gonna make us breakfast?"

"Yeah." I rub my stomach. "I woke up hungry."

The narrow basement steps lead to a small laundry room, where salamanders sometimes run, and another room we call the food cellar, where I keep all the jars of fruits and vegetables I've preserved and pails of sand with fresh vegetables such as carrots, potatoes, and turnips. Toivo keeps his deep freeze down here, too. When times are good, it's full of fish and meat— walleye, grouse, duck, pheasant, turkey, venison, and bear. When times are rough, like they were before Toivo got the turkey yesterday, the freezer looks like an old man's toothless mouth.

I ignore the large pile of dirty clothes next to the washing machine. Instead, from a pail in a dark corner,

I pull out four groundnuts, which look like small, knobby potatoes. They grow underground on long roots, spreading out like baubles on a necklace.

Back upstairs, I put a teaspoon of instant Folgers in a cup and fill it with rusty tap water. I go to put it in the microwave when Toivo says, "It's broke."

"Oh," I say.

"I heat mine up in a saucepan," he says.

So I dump my coffee into the saucepan and turn on the gas and ignite the stove. I put a pot of water on the stove to boil. Then I dab some butter in a frying pan and set the burner to low.

I notice that Mikko's and Alexi's round and lumpy backpacks sit nearby on the floor. "Guess I better check if the boys had homework we forgot to do last night," I say.

Toivo adjusts his hearing aid. "What?" he says.

I repeat myself.

"Good idea," Toivo says. He sips his coffee, but he doesn't make a move to open the backpacks.

First, I open Mom's recipe book.

With a sharp paring knife, I flick the peelings off the groundnuts and soften them up in the boiling water. Once they are ready, I slice a few petals off the mushroom and toss it all into the melted butter.

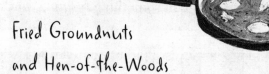

Fried Groundnuts
and Hen-of-the-Woods

Harvest a large mushroom. Separate the petals. Brush them clean with a toothbrush. Look out for any worms or weevils living in the mushroom. But don't worry too much, because even if you miss a few, eating them won't kill you. Boil water. Toss in peeled groundnuts until soft. Remove and slice like you would a potato.

Dab a tablespoon of butter in a heavy fry pan. Get the butter and pan nice and hot. Then slip the mushrooms and groundnuts in. Brown them for a few minutes. Pour an egg-and-milk mixture over the groundnuts and mushrooms. Fry for another minute. Feeds 6.

"Do you smell smoke?" Toivo asks me. Deep, dark circles stress his eyes.

I sniff. "Well," I say, "I smell gas from the stove. And butter. But I do smell something burning, too." I sniff again.

The windows rattle as another semi loaded with piping from Grandpa's factory barrels down our road toward the woods.

Toivo scoops up most of the envelopes and heads outside for the mailbox. Two unopened envelopes have been abandoned on the table. One is from Grandpa's lawyer. The other is from Children's Protective Services. I slide them under the plate that holds the napkins and salt and pepper. I don't want to see them, either.

Toivo's phone vibrates and lights up with BIG JOHN. Grandpa.

I don't want to talk to him, but I don't want Grandpa leaving a nasty message on Toivo's phone, either. So I flip open the phone and say "Hello?"

"Johanna?" Grandpa says.

Oh no. He thinks I'm Mom.

"Oh, Fern. Fern." Grandpa's words are muffled.

"I'm sorry, Fern. You just sound so much like your mother....I forgot for a second." He takes a slobbery breath, and I hope he doesn't start crying.

"That's okay, Grandpa." My eyes burn, but I look down at the floor and try to think about something else. No one's ever said I sound like Mom before. A lot of people tell me I look just like she did. That makes me happy, I guess. Except that when I look in the mirror, all I see are gigantic alien eyes.

A few seconds pass. It'd be hard to imagine a big guy like my grandpa weeping, but he does. I've seen him. But Grandpa has a knack for doing something that makes you mad at him all over again in a hurry.

"How are you?" I finally ask him.

He allows a few more seconds to pass while he composes himself. "I'm fine, Fern. How are you?" He sounds tired and grumpy, like an overworked old mule, the kind you think is safe to pet but will bite your hand off if you try.

"Fine."

It's silent again. I don't know why two people who share the same blood can have so little to talk about, but that's how it is with Grandpa. He adds, "That's good to hear. And how are the boys? Are they keeping up in school?"

"Um…" I cradle the phone between my ear and shoulder. I unzip Mikko's and Alexi's school bags and tip them upside down. Baseballs bounce out. Animal bones rattle to the floor. Banana peels slither on their own decaying gel. Mismatched gloves tumble. Soggy motocross magazines flutter out. And pocketknives, unsleeved, stab the floor at my toes. I'll have to talk to them about the pocketknives. Even though having one is normal for boys around here, I know there's a school rule against them.

I shake each bag just to make sure there's nothing else in there. A lone school paper floats to the floor. Spelling test. He scored 6/10.

"Yeah," I say. "Alexi just did really great on his spelling test."

"Oh, that's good to hear. Seems I got a call about his spelling tests from his teacher not too long ago. Glad to hear he's doing better." Alexi's teacher and Grandpa's secretary are best friends. They are also the two biggest gossips in town.

"Yep," I say. "He is."

"And you?"

"Um…I'm doing pretty good, too."

"My company just donated a nice prize to the STEM fair," he says. "I hope you have a good project idea that you're working on."

My face feels hot, and more of my hair is probably turning gray. "I better get the boys ready for school now, Grandpa."

"I bought a pair of Jet Skis for you and the boys to take out on the lake next summer."

"I saw a truck with a bunch of your pipes on it," I say.

"Oh yes!" His voice brightens up. "We secured a very good contract with Kloche's. And once they get Millner off his land and start clearing those woods, you just watch the jobs come back to Colter."

"Wait," I say. "What about Millner's woods?" I bite a fingernail.

"Kloche's is going to put a wastewater pond there. That darn Millner has got to go."

Millner used to work for Grandpa. Until the accident. Then Grandpa fired him. Getting Horace Millner out of my life sounds good to me. But not the "clearing those woods" part.

I spit my torn fingernail onto the floor. "You mean Kloche wants to cut down the trees? The ones around our property?"

"Of course!" says Grandpa. "They have to. They have to put the fracking wastewater somewhere!"

Fracking again. *Drilling miles and miles beneath the surface*, Mr. Flores said. *Wastewater pond*, he said. I'm trying to imagine the trees gone and a big scummy pond in its place. Where will I find mushrooms or white onions? "B-but," I stutter. "But what about—"

"Now, Fern," he interrupts, "don't you worry. I'm getting you out of there. I've got lots of trees and toys for you here."

Grandpa's property is surrounded by ornamental trees, perfectly pruned and perfectly spaced, not my idea of a woods. Woods should be wild, with animal trails and bird fights and overgrown plants.

"I like it here," I tell him, my voice shaking. I look around the kitchen and try to think up a reason to get off the phone.

"Is Toivo around? I have to speak with him." Grandpa's voice has changed. He's all boss now.

I decide to change my tone, too. "No." I clear my

throat and lower my chin. "He's not available right now. May I take a message?"

A few seconds pass. "I see," he says. "No, no. That won't be necessary. I'll try him again later."

"I think he's pretty busy all day."

Grandpa guffaws. "I doubt that." In my imagination, I can see his six-foot-six frame lean forward and jab a finger in my face. "That man is the sorriest excuse—"

"Okay," I interrupt. "I have to get ready for school now. Bye." Then I close the phone. I exhale real long and wait for my heart to stop kicking.

I can't let him scare me. Who does he think he is? So what if he has a big voice? So what if he has a lot of money? So what if he's the owner of Greene Incorporated? So what if practically everyone works for him? So what if he has supper and takes vacations with politicians? He can't just have his way all the time.

Can he?

He didn't get his way with Mom. She chose Toivo over her father's money. I choose Toivo over Grandpa's money, too.

Or at least I want to. But Children's Protective Services might have other ideas.

The boys twist down the stairs and dust-devil into the kitchen.

"Where's Dad?" says Mikko. "We're sick." He places the back of his palm against his forehead and closes his eyes as though he feels faint.

"Yeah," says Alexi, who is walking with his arms in front of him like a mummy risen from the dead. "We don't want to go to school."

"Don't even try it," I say. I fork a groundnut from the frying pan to test it. Just right. Then I use it to point at Mikko. "You're not sick. And you *are* going to school."

"Daaaad!" they yell. Mikko forces a fake cough. Alexi holds his stomach and moans.

"I know you had homework," I say to him. "Did you bring it home? I looked in your backpack and couldn't find it. Where is it?" Alexi is in first grade for the second time. This is Mikko's first try at third grade, but it's not going too well.

They hug and slap each other's backs and collapse on the floor, rowdy with laughter, which turns into a roly-poly battle of punches and kicking. Mikko's skinny legs strike at Alexi's body. Alexi's elbows shoot jabs into Mikko's middle.

"Ouch!" Mikko shouts. He curls up into a ball. "You got me in the jewels!"

"You don't have any jewels!" Alexi says.

"Well then, no breakfast for you," I tell them.

"All right," says Mikko, and fishes a folded-up piece of math homework from his back pocket. Alexi pulls flash cards out from under the couch cushion. They settle at the table with their homework. Mikko's eyes slide up and to the right, like he's trying to find an answer he hid behind his ear. Alexi chews on the eraser end of his pencil while I serve up breakfast.

Toivo opens the screen door. The boys run to him and cling to his legs and whine about their imaginary illnesses. When Toivo checks with me, I shake my head.

"Well," he says, "it looks like these boys are very sick, Fernny. I guess I'll have to give them the special medicine." Toivo makes a natural concoction for headaches, nausea, chills, and what have you. I don't know for sure, but I think one of the ingredients is deer urine. It smells like rotten tree bark and tastes like a possum's tail. I would know because I have eaten possum.

The boys look at each other with widened eyes and round mouths. Alexi pinches his nose closed.

"Oh yes. I think a dose of the special medicine is

just what they need." I grab Mikko's arms and hold them behind his back. "Open up!" Toivo goes to the cupboard and pulls out an old milk jug filled with his special medicine. Mikko strains to get away from me. He stomps on my foot.

"Ow!" I shout.

"I feel better," he says. "And I'm hungry." I drop his arms.

"Me, too," says Alexi. They scramble to the table.

Toivo puts the medicine back in the cupboard, and I giggle and then join the boys.

Toivo eats real slowly. "Boys, chew your food. Don't gulp." He rarely enforces rules, but he insists that we eat slowly and appreciate the work that has gone into providing and preparing it. "Fernny, you are the best cook I know." His chin glistens.

After we finish breakfast, Toivo wrestles socks onto the boys' feet while I toss the dishes into the sink, which is already full of dirty pots and pans, when a car pulls into the driveway.

"Who could that be?" I ask. I glance at the house, all messy with filthy clothes, dust, and toys everywhere.

Toivo goes to the window and separates the blinds to have a look. "Uh-oh."

Chapter 5

When you live protected by branches and leaves, you favor privacy. Unexpected visitors might even make you edgy. In our case, unexpected visitors often mean the electricity company wants a check or a repo man wants to take Toivo's truck because he hasn't paid the bills.

Once, a visitor on an early morning a lot like this one turned into a sheriff standing on our stoop, gesturing Toivo outside, putting his arm around Toivo's shoulders, and whispering to him quietly as he looked back toward me and Mikko and Alexi.

"Who is it?" I ask Toivo. He shushes me.

There's a knock on the door. It reminds me of that sheriff's knock on the door, the one that led to news that brought Toivo to his knees.

Toivo puts one hand over each of the boys' mouths. "Shhh," he says. "Get down!"

I crouch on the kitchen floor next to where Toivo and the boys are slouched.

"Who are we hiding from?" I whisper.

"*Hello?*" comes a woman's voice from behind the door. *Rap, rap, rap.* "Mr. Heikkenen?"

Our door is so thin that we can hear her muttering to herself. "Now where did I put that paper?"

Then she yells through the door, "Mr. Toivo?" We can hear papers fluttering, and more mumbling. "What kind of a name is that? Which of these is his first name?"

Now she's speaking up again. "Mr. Toivo Heikkenen, are you in there? Mr. Heikkenen Toivo! I know this is unexpected, but I had another case just up the road, and I've been trying to catch you at home for so long, so I thought I'd stop by."

We hear sounds like briefcase latches unsnapping. "Let me see here," she says to herself. "I know it's here somewhere...."

Rap, rap, rap. "It's Miss Tassel, Mr. Toivo. The court has appointed me to your case. We need to schedule the home inspection."

She drops something that lands with a thud on the porch. "Oh, shoot." Another thud of something dropping. "For crying out loud, I'm wearing two different shoes!"

Toivo rolls his eyes. The boys put their own hands over Toivo's hands, which are still covering their mouths. Their wild eyes are watering with laughter.

"Okay, then," she calls. There's more shuffling and scratching. A business card slips under the crack in the door. Nobody moves to get it.

The *clack, click, clack, click* of her mismatched shoes takes her back to her car. We creep up to the window and peer out.

Miss Tassel is short, but she has at least a foot of hair curling off her head. She opens the passenger side of her tan Caprice Classic. Papers and a plastic coffee cup fall out onto the ground. She throws in her briefcase and quickly gathers up the trash and tosses it back into the car before she gets in.

When she turns the ignition, the car goes *click* and *tick* and then quiets.

"Starter's bad," says Toivo. He chews on the corner of his thumbnail.

She tries again. *Tick. Tick. Tick.* Miss Tassel smacks the dashboard with her bare hand.

"That's not going to help," Toivo says.

Almost as if she's heard Toivo, Miss Tassel leans back in her seat and crosses herself, then presses her hands together in prayer. She closes her eyes and moves her lips.

"That's not going to help, either," I say.

"You got that right," says Toivo.

Miss Tassel rolls down the window to listen to the engine as she turns the ignition key. She's clenching the steering wheel and standing on the accelerator. "Come on! Help me, Jesus. Come on! Come on!"

Mikko and Alexi are laughing full on now.

"Good grief," says Toivo. He stands up. "Grab my hammer, Mikko," he says.

"Yay!" screams Mikko. He dashes off to grab the hammer out of Toivo's tool bag, which rests next to the couch.

"Yippee!" shouts Alexi. "Are we going to break her windows?"

"No!" scolds Toivo.

"Her bumper?" asks Mikko. He hands the hammer to Toivo and looks up at him with hopeful eyes.

Toivo runs his hand through his thin hair. "Boys, I'm going to fix her car, not wreck it." Toivo used to work as a mechanic at the motor company before the factory closed up and a lot of people in town lost their jobs.

He squeezes my shoulder. "I guess the jig is up. Fernny, finish getting the boys ready for school."

Before you know it, Toivo's shimmied under the front of Miss Tassel's car to give the starter a whack. Before I close the door, Mikko sniffs. "Smells like smoke out there," he says.

I smell it, too. Suddenly, my heart drops. "What did Miss Tassel say?" I ask the boys. "Did she say something about being 'just up the road'?"

The boys ignore me while they stuff their feet into their shoes. Alexi's big toe sticks out of a hole in his.

"Hurry up, guys," I say. "Let's go." I weave their arms through the straps of their backpacks and shove them out the door.

Miss Tassel stands near the bumper of her car. Toivo's legs stick out from underneath it.

"Hi, kids!" She's got a great big smile on that looks sincere but makes me nervous.

"Hi," I say.

"On your way to school?" she asks. She crosses her arms, then uncrosses them. Maybe she's nervous, too.

"Yeah, but we've got to pick up our neighbors first."

Her smile tightens. She points up the road with long pink fingernails. "You mean those children who live over there?"

In the direction she's pointing, thin strands of black smoke curl in the dusty pink sky. "Mark-Richard and Gary? Yeah."

Toivo slithers out from underneath the car. "That should do it."

Miss Tassel moves out of Toivo's way. "The kids aren't there this morning. I just came from there. The smoke…" She hesitates.

"What?" says Toivo. "What is it?"

Miss Tassel leans over and whispers to Toivo, "It's from their house."

"Mark-Richard! Is he okay?" I ask.

Miss Tassel puffs her cheeks. "I shouldn't have told you that—but, yes, everyone is fine. The boys got out of the house without getting hurt."

Toivo wipes gravel off his jeans. "I should get over there and lend a hand...."

"No one's there," says Miss Tassel. "I just stopped over to see if I could salvage some of the kids' things and get some comfort items to them."

"Where?" I say. "Where are they?"

Miss Tassel moves gravel around with the tip of her shoe. "You're going to have to talk with Mark-Richard, I'm afraid," she says. "I can't tell you that."

"But when?" I ask. "Today?"

"No," she says. "Not today."

"Did you take him and Gary away from their parents?"

"Fern," Toivo warns.

"Did you?" I demand, more loudly than I intended.

Miss Tassel tilts her head the way adults sometimes do when they're telling kids things they don't want to hear. "It's complicated, Fern."

I start down the driveway. "Come on, boys," I shout to Mikko and Alexi. They listen for once and follow behind me. Both boys stare lightning and axes and hot lava at Miss Tassel. "We don't want you to come here anymore!" I add, and start running, with the boys keeping pace.

We keep running toward Mark-Richard's house.

After a while, Alexi calls out, "Ferrrrn, slow down!" He sits in the middle of the road, forcing me to slow down, then stop.

"Come on!" I walk back toward him. "Up! You can't sit here. You'll get hit by a truck."

"My legs feel like licorice. Why are we running away from that lady? Is she bad?"

"She's a witch," says Mikko. "She took Mark-Richard and Gary away. Now we can't be friends with them anymore."

I pull Alexi to his feet and dust him off. "They'll be back."

But I'm not sure they will.

All is completely still and quiet. No wild turkeys, coyotes, white-tailed deer, spiky porcupines, corn snakes, or any other woodsy creatures. The silence is eerie, as though everything is hiding and holding its breath.

The smoke gets denser the closer we get. "Boys, walk next to me." I pull them by their backpacks to either side of my body.

Mikko twists and fights. "Knock it off, Fern!"

"Shhh," I hush them. "Listen! Listen to the woods."

Mikko cups a hand around his ear, and Alexi pauses.

"I don't hear anything," Alexi says.

"I know," I say. "It's weird."

"Maybe the fire scared all the animals away," says Mikko.

I shrug my shoulders. "Yeah, maybe."

We take light steps on the gravel road. Soon Mark-Richard's driveway is in sight. The smoke becomes denser, but not choking. Mark-Richard's house wasn't much more than four thin walls of plywood. The fire probably burned out fast.

At his driveway, we stop. Only the skeleton of their trailer—four upright boards and a small section of the floor—remains, scorched black. Off to one side of the charred house is a pile of toys and clothes and a mattress the firefighters must have saved. The woods between our houses are thick, but I can't believe I didn't even hear sirens.

Alexi leans into me. He puts his thumb in his mouth. I don't tell him to quit being a baby.

Mikko inhales sharply. He grabs my hand. His is damp and icy cold. He points at the garbage pile. "Look."

A black bear stands up and spies us.

He's at least six feet tall. His coat is shaggy and dull

and black as cast iron. The kind we call "dump bears" is what he is. They show up every now and then, when they can't find enough to eat in the woods, to eat people's garbage or drink from their rain barrels. He must have frightened all the other animals away.

"Don't. Move," I whisper. Usually, when news of a bear wandering around gets out, people continue about their ordinary business with a few extra precautions. Don't let little pets outside. Carry bear spray.

I don't have bear spray.

Mikko steps behind me and whimpers. Alexi takes the thumb out of his mouth, leans down, and picks up a stone.

"Don't!" I scold. The bear huffs, angry at us for interrupting him. He drops to all fours and then stands up again. He smashes aside rubbish with his two front paws.

We gasp and step back. I clutch Alexi to me and reach behind me to hold on to Mikko, too.

"Fern?" Mikko cries.

Alexi winds up and throws the stone toward the bear. "Go away!" he shouts.

"Alexi, *no*!"

But it's too late. The stone hits the bear near his eye

and drops to the ground. The bear roars and swipes at the stone, flinging up clumps of gravel. He leaves deep claw marks in the earth. Then he drops to all fours again and steps toward us.

"When I say 'run,'" I tell the boys, without moving my mouth, "you run and don't stop until you reach the water tower."

The boys breathe hard. I scan the ground for something to protect us. Then, out of the woods, I see a flash of fur running toward the bear.

The bear shakes his giant head.

A dog opens his jaws. His gritty bark snaps the air.

Ranger.

"Run!" I say. My brothers scramble off behind me. "Run!" I turn and watch them until they are safely down the driveway.

Ranger and the bear snarl at each other. The bear takes swipes at Ranger. Ranger gnashes his teeth at the bear.

I walk backward and watch. The bear turns sideways and shakes his coat. Ranger keeps his gaze fixed on him. The dog's whole body seems pointed like a dart. The bear turns back once more and roars at Ranger, and then he saunters off into the woods.

After he's disappeared, Ranger sits down but keeps watch.

When I catch up with the boys, I wrap them both up in giant hugs.

"Gross," says Mikko, but he squeezes me back. "That bear was going to eat us! But that wolf saved us."

"Ranger isn't a wolf," I say. "He's a dog."

"Is he yours?" asks Alexi. "Where did you get him? Why didn't you share? Why do you get to name him?"

"He's not mine. I just know him." I notice that the sun is high. "We're going to be late. Come on."

Toivo likes to tell a story about Mom even though he wasn't there when it happened. He just retells it from the way she told it to him. Once when I was small, Mom took me for a walk. She put me in the stroller. Out of nowhere, a Doberman dashed out from woods and made a beeline for me. Its fangs dripped with madness. That's how Toivo tells it anyway.

Mom stepped in front of me just as the dog leaped for my face. The dog jumped up on her, ready to bite, but she shoved her thumbs into either hinge of the dog's jaw and pushed them down into the Doberman's throat. Then she heaved the dog backward. It landed on its back. Got up. Put its tail between its legs and slunk away, whimpering.

That's the kind of mom she was.

I don't know what I would have done had Ranger not come and distracted that bear. But I'd like to think that I would have protected my brothers the way Mom protected me.

Chapter 6

As if seeing the bear wasn't enough excitement for one morning, there's more up ahead. Red and blue lights flash.

My brothers dash toward a cop car. A police officer has one of Kloche's trucks pulled over. The officer is standing on the road, writing out a ticket.

"You truckers have *got* to slow down," I hear him say to the driver. "This *is not* a demolition derby. You're going to kill somebody!" He tears the ticket from a pad and reaches it up to the truck driver.

"Sir," the trucker says, "I understand your position, but you should take it up with our boss. We get paid by the load, and we got to *move* these pipes. The boss says he'll replace me in a second if I don't make ten runs a day!"

The officer shakes his head at the trucker.

"Was he bad?" Mikko asks the cop. "Are you going to arrest him?"

"Can I help?" asks Alexi. "Can I do the cuffs?"

The cop ignores them and checks his watch. "Hey, you kids better hurry. Bell's about to ring." He uses his thumb to point toward the school.

"Yes, sir," I say. "Sorry, sir." I push Mikko and Alexi out ahead of me.

Alexi darts away from me and toward the officer. Before I can call him back, he's telling the officer, "Give him a ticket for making the road all gloopy and for waking me up all the time, too."

The truck driver releases some kind of air pressure from his brakes that drowns Alexi out. The police officer leans down, pats Alexi on the head, and turns him back around toward me.

"When I grow up, I'm going to be a cop and give tickets to all those guys all day long," he tells me.

"That's great, Alexi," I tell him. "But first you have to pass elementary school."

When we get to school, I drop the boys off at their classrooms and then head to mine. Even though it's well past eight, Mr. Flores hasn't started class yet. He doesn't even look up from his laptop when I come in.

Alkomso glances up at me from her reading, then at the clock, and shakes her head. Of course, she's going ahead of the chapters we were assigned in *Hatchet*. Her English wasn't very good when she first moved to Colter, but now her best class is English. Whenever there's a writing contest at school, Alkomso wins.

She smacks the book shut and cleaves it to her chest. "The next chapter is so exciting," she says. "Brian gets caught up in a tornado. I'm dying to see a tornado. I can't believe I've lived here four years, and still nothing!"

I want to tell her about the bear or Mark-Richard, but she keeps talking. "I hope he meets a girl out there in the wilderness. Wouldn't that be a great plot twist?" Alkomso opens the book again and flips ahead a few more chapters, skimming the pages.

Alkomso talks about love, marriage, and babies a lot. She wants to be a romance novelist one day. Sometimes it drives me kind of crazy. But she doesn't have as many things to worry about as I do.

Other than her love of love, we have a lot in common. Neither of us has a phone. Neither of us listens to the music everyone else does. We both have unusual families. Her dad is a taxi driver in a city four hours away. He stays there for four or five days and then comes home for a few days, then goes back to work. Her mom takes care of the kids and home while he's gone.

Margot and her friends are smelling each other's hair. "New shampoo," says Margot. "Green-apple scented." She looks over at Alkomso. "Sometimes I wish I could be like Alkomso and not ever have to wash my hair. I wish I could keep it covered up all the time, so no one would ever know if I did or didn't wash my hair." Margot's often got a snake tongue, but lately she's been extra venomous.

Alkomso pushes her chair back as though she's going to stand up and let Margot have it. But before she can, Mr. Flores stands. "Okay, okay," he says. "Boring business stuff first." He picks up the attendance pad and scans the heads in the room, stopping at Mark-Richard's empty desk and chair. "Hey, where's my main man, Mark-Richard?"

Margot raises her hand and flails it around. "Mr. Flores, I know where he is."

"Where's that?" Mr. Flores scratches his head with the pencil.

"In foster care," she says, acting proud that she has inside information. "Mark-Richard burned his own house down." She rolls her eyes like Mark-Richard is the biggest idiot on the planet.

"What?!" Mr. Flores says.

"Shut up, Margot," says Alkomso.

But Margot keeps talking. "Mark-Richard's mom ran away. So Mark-Richard's dad went to bring her back home."

Sometimes I wish Margot would fall into a snake pit. I give her my worst dirty look.

"Don't look at me like that, Fern," she says. "You're probably just worried because everyone knows you might be taken away next."

My face burns.

Alkomso slaps her desk. "I mean it, Margot. You better be quiet."

"*Hey!*" shouts Mr. Flores. "Knock it off!"

I'm furious and curious and scared all at once. I want Margot to shut up, too, but I also want to know what happened.

"How did he burn his house down?" asks another kid.

Margot puffs up with importance. "Well," she says, "my mom says that Mark-Richard sat his cat on the couch and put a candle flame to a wood tick on its ear. But Mark-Richard didn't know that his mom had doused the couch in kerosene to kill bedbugs. The cat leaped off the couch, knocked the candle out of Mark-Richard's hands, and up went the flames. Mark-Richard got Gary and the cat out, and they all got picked up by the county lady."

That would be Miss Tassel.

"Poor Mark-Richard," Alkomso whispers.

"Yeah," I say. "I saw the house this morning."

"Oh no!" says Mr. Flores. "I wish I had known. I'd adopt that little guy in two seconds."

Margot taps the toe of her shoe on the floor. "You can't do that, Mr. Flores," she says. "My mom says you have to have a nice house to have children. You can't just live out of a camper."

Margot's mom has been trying to get Mr. Flores fired because he showed us a video filmed inside a hogging operation where all the pigs were full of sores and dying from disease and mistreatment. Margot Peterson's dad owns the fifth-largest hogging operation in the country.

Mr. Flores sighs. "Let's move on to the next thing—topics for the STEM fair. Has everyone decided on theirs?"

"I have," Margot says. "I'm going to make a volcano."

"Booor-ing," says Mr. Flores. "Pick something else. Really think. Think about something that affects you or your family or your community."

Mr. Flores explains that the STEM fair will be held at the end of the month, and parents and neighbors are invited to attend. He asks a few other kids and writes some topic ideas on the whiteboard and nearly loses his mind with excitement when one boy says he's going to take apart a carburetor and explain how it works.

"Awesome," he says. "I dig it completely. I love when I get to learn something from you brainiacs."

"I'm think I'm doing fracking," Alkomso says. "My dad is getting a new job with Kloche's, so he can be closer to home."

The corners of Mr. Flores's mouth turn down. Then he opens his mouth, but no words come out.

"He is?" I say. "Why didn't you tell me?"

Alkomso shrugs. "I just found out this morning. He starts in a few weeks. My mom is so happy. And

Dad says he'll have more time to help out around the house." Alkomso has a new little sister. Kaltumo is her name. She's pretty much the cutest thing I've ever seen. She's also a lot of work.

But that means that Alkomso's dad will be working for the company that plans to put the wastewater pond right in Millner's woods.

"What about my grove?" I say to Alkomso. "Kloche's wants to cut it all down."

"Well, my family needs my dad home more."

"But my family needs the woods for food."

Alkomso and I stare into each other's eyes. Several seconds pass.

Margot coughs a fake cough. "My dad says fracking is going to bring lots of new jobs to Colter," she says. "Fern, maybe your dad should just get a job with Kloche's, too."

Alkomso's eyes widen. Mine do, too. It's almost like, for a brief second, Alkomso and Margot are on the same side.

And I am on the other side. I turn around in my chair and face the front.

"Fern?" says Mr. Flores.

My face gets hot. I hate being called on. "Yeah?"

"Your project. Have you decided on one?"

"I don't know yet," I mumble.

"You keep thinking." He points at me with his pen. "I know you'll think of something great. You're a born naturalist."

I muster a tight smile. I don't know what a naturalist is exactly, but it sounds like someone who loves the outdoors.

"Anyway, let's move on and hit the bird-watching trail. Everybody ready?" He puts a pair of binoculars around his neck.

Alkomso stands and pushes in her chair. "This is going to be so fun, isn't it?"

I try my best to smile.

"Are you mad at me because my dad got that job?" she asks. "Because you shouldn't be. Everything is going to be fine."

I nod even if I don't believe it. "I'm not mad at you. I just have a lot on my mind." I look over at Mark-Richard's empty desk. "I feel bad for Mark-Richard."

"Me, too," she says. "But he'll be back, I'm sure."

She puts her arm around my shoulder. It feels heavy.

Chapter 7

Once the final bell rings, I go to Mikko's and Alexi's classrooms to pick them up. Alexi's teacher, the one who is best friends with Grandpa's secretary, stops me. She tells me something about Alexi having to get a consequence today for fidgeting around and being a distraction.

How's he supposed to sit still when his best friend has been taken away and he was nearly attacked by a bear this morning? is what I want to say.

"Okay," I tell her instead. She keeps yapping about him needing to learn to stay in his seat and such. Though her mouth barely moves, all these words keep spilling out of it. She's got a loose double chin that hangs from her jaw.

"Yep," I tell her. "Got it."

She wraps her bony fingers around my arm. I yank it away. "I put a report in his backpack. Make sure his father reads it. If he knows how to read, that is." Then she spins on her heel and turns away to target another kid.

I give Alexi's hand a little squeeze. He smiles up at me.

"She looks like a toad," he says a little too loudly.

I am proud to be his sister. And Mikko's, too. I don't care what those stupid papers say about my brothers and their bad behavior, even if some of it's true.

On the way home, we make lots of noise as we pass Mark-Richard's house, since noise usually keeps bears away. There's just the slightest whiff of smoke.

I wonder where Mark-Richard is now. When you've spent so many days of your life walking to and from school with someone, you get to know that person pretty well. Especially when that person lives kind of in the wild, like I do. Mark-Richard is a good friend. I wish I had told him that yesterday, when I had the chance.

When we get to a stand of beech trees, I stop and stare at the golden canopy, thinking I'd like to bring some of the nuts home. Roasted beechnuts are tasty. And beechnut butter on homemade bread with a glass of warm milk is a treat Mom would sometimes give us before bed.

I look up and down the road and into Millner's woods, but I don't see a soul. I listen. All the regular animal activity is back, which makes me sure the bear has moved on. So I climb over the fence, and the boys crawl under, following me. We walk to the biggest beech trunk, mottled gray and smooth.

The wind dies down. Mom's presence is all around. She brought us out here all the time, spring, summer, fall, and winter. There was always something new to discover. Baby ducks following their mom at the pond. Nettles after the first thaw. Little fawns learning how to walk in spring. Wild grapes in August. Pheasant's back mushrooms around harvest. Pine needles for tea on the short days of winter. *Somebody should make a list of all the good food to be found in these woods*, she'd say. Back then there was no reason to be afraid of Millner. He was just our neighbor, a regular nobody-special like us.

I wish I could talk to Mom and ask all the questions I have about what's happening with Toivo, Grandpa, Kloche's, and Mark-Richard. I try to let all those scary thoughts go. Right now I just want to enjoy that protected and calm sense I had when I was around Mom.

And when I decide to dump the bad thoughts, she surrounds me again. I feel safe. I don't know if there's an afterlife. It's not a topic we've ever really talked about at home, but somehow right now it feels as though there is.

When a tender wind finally rustles the branches, a few beechnuts hit the ground. Mikko opens his backpack and begins tossing them in. Alexi and I kneel down and help.

When our bags are about half-full, a whiny howl breaks the silence. We all stop and pop up our heads.

Owwww-ooooooo! it goes again.

"What's that?" asks Alexi.

Ow-ow-oooooo!

We stand, and I move the boys behind me, sheltering them between me and the tree.

And then we hear footsteps coming toward us.

Alexi and Mikko grab hold of my arm and squeeze

tight. I lean down and pick up an old heavy stick. I hold it out in front of us.

"Who's there?" I demand.

Ow-ooooooo. The noise sounds low and lonely.

I turn. The footsteps come steadily. At last, from the depths of the woods, I see Ranger.

He's hanging his head so that his nose nearly touches the ground. He walks a few more feet and then sits, keeping his head down.

It's then that I see what he's whining about. Around his neck dangles a dead mallard duck.

"Oh, Ranger," I whisper. "What did you do?" The emerald-green head of the mallard, a drake, hangs from a leash of twine tied tight behind Ranger's head.

"He killed it!" says Mikko. He's pointing at Ranger as if the dog is in a police lineup.

"He's getting a consequence!" says Alexi.

Ranger lowers his head in shame.

Around here, if a dog kills a chicken, goose, or duck, the owner ties the dead fowl around the dog's neck until the bird decays and falls off. The dog has to live with, and smell, the result of his bad deed. That way, the dog learns not to attack the birds again. The best dogs learn to protect, not harm, them.

Ranger's eyes peel the ground. He whines as though in sorrow.

"Did you kill that duck, Ranger?" I say. I'm somewhere between angry and disbelieving.

The weight of the plump bird has already pulled so tight on the twine leash that Ranger's skin is chafing, and in one place an open wound, cut by the rope, is bleeding. Ranger sits back and scratches at the duck and the leash, but to no avail. The leash is attached securely to the mallard and to him.

"That's not fair," says Mikko. "He didn't do it on purpose."

I sigh. "We don't know if he did or didn't. But if he did, I'm sure it couldn't be helped." I crouch down and lock eyes with the dog. He is a pile of misery and shame. "Being a hunter is in his nature." I wonder how I'm going to get close to Ranger.

I remember dumping the boys' pocketknives out of their bags. "Does one of you guys still have a pocketknife in your backpack?"

Both boys dive into their bags and swim around in the depths until they both pull out knives. What I should be doing is scolding them for carrying pocketknives to school, but right now I'm really glad they have them.

"I'll do it," says Mikko.

"I want to do it," says Alexi.

I take Mikko's. "*I'll* do it," I tell them. "You boys sit still and be quiet. I don't want to startle Ranger."

Down on all fours, I crawl very, very slowly toward Ranger. Toivo taught me that you shouldn't make eye contact with wild or hurt animals, that eye contact makes them think you're challenging them. So I let my hair fall over my face and create two curtains over my eyes. I can see a little bit through the hair. When I get close, he stands up and looks back toward where he came from, as though searching for an escape route. I stop.

"It's okay," I tell him. "I'm not going to hurt you."

He licks his nose, then breathes with his tongue hanging out. He sits again, uses a back leg to try to scratch off the duck. The duck shakes wildly but doesn't come loose. Ranger stops and moans.

I crawl again until I'm close enough to reach out and touch him. The rotting-duck scent hits my nose. My stomach turns, sending bile up into my mouth. I swallow it back down and turn my head to get a breath of fresh air.

"Oh, Ranger," I say. "Don't worry. We're going to get that off you."

I reach out gingerly. Ranger growls softly, but I don't think he's really mad, only scared. I keep whispering to him.

Finally, I have my fingertips on his fur, near his neck. His eyes slip to the side in an attempt to see my hand, but he doesn't move.

"It's okay," I keep whispering.

He growls again. A little louder this time.

"Get away from him," says Mikko.

"He's gonna bite you," says Alexi.

"Shhh," I say to them. Truth is, I am a little nervous.

Ranger peels back his lips a bit, showing his long, sharp teeth. I swallow, but I carefully put more of my hand on his fur.

I slip my fingertips between the rope and Ranger's neck. I guide the knife tip to the twine.

Ranger snarls. I jump back and drop the knife.

Ranger stands up and circles around. He shakes his head wildly, trying to detach the duck. The duck flails but remains attached to Ranger's neck. He groans.

"Just leave him," says Alexi. "He's going to bite you and give you scabies!"

"Not *scabies*, you dumb diarrhea-head," says Mikko. "Arthritis!"

"Yeah, arthritis."

"Rabies, you mean," I say to them. "But Ranger doesn't have rabies."

I reach for the knife again. This time I don't worry about eye contact. If Ranger wanted to attack me, he would have already.

Ranger sits, and then he lies down in the leaves, putting his head on his front legs. He sighs.

"That's right," I say. "Just relax."

I creep next to him, and he lifts his eyes to me. They're soft and accepting, not suspicious. I slip the knife between his neck and the twine again and begin sawing. Four or five cuts, and the rope separates. The duck drops to the forest floor.

Ranger jumps up, barks, and runs around and around in big circles. He leaps, biting at bees and butterflies. He snags a stick and carries it like a flag. He's wild and free.

"You did it! You did it, Fernny!" says Mikko.

"You are the best sister in the whole world!" says Alexi.

"Go, Ranger!" I laugh.

Ranger stops. He barks high and happy, then bolts through the trees, back where he came from.

"Now we're even!" I shout after him. But he's long gone.

Chapter 8

The TV babbles in the living room. Toivo's at the computer, a relic hand-me-down. His face glows as job postings fly by. When he sees something interesting, he jabs at the computer keys with his pointer fingers. Once in a while, he looks up and asks me questions: "Fernny, do you think I could be a dentist's receptionist? How about a bank teller? Here's one! A professional dancer in a reputable establishment! Can you see me working there? Shaking my money-maker?" He stands up and wiggles around. The boys join in, wiggling their arms and legs like they've been stung by hornets.

For years, Toivo worked as a mechanic at the auto plant, until the company moved the operation to Mexico. After that he tried work as a janitor, until the office building closed. Then as a truck driver, until he couldn't pass the written test. He did a stint as a laborer at a hog farm, until the operator started hiring immigrants because he could pay them practically nothing. He got a job as a gas station attendant, until the manager hired a teenager who would work practically for free. Then as a bartender, until the bar owner couldn't afford to pay the liquor tax and the place got shut down. Then he was a small-engine repairman, until the work got so slow that he got laid off. These days he does odd jobs for cash.

I set aside the beechnuts I've been shelling. "Okay, boys. Now let's get this homework done."

Mikko and Alexi scurry under the kitchen table. They curl into balls and take turns covering each other as though I'm a monster who's going to eat them.

I lean over and peer under the table. "Come on." I swipe my arm at them. "Come out from under there."

"You can't make us," Mikko says. He purses his lips.

"I don't even have any homework," says Alexi. He sticks his tongue out at me.

"Baloney!" I shout.

My patience is short. I have to think up a project for the STEM fair, and I'm starting to get nervous about it. Maybe if I had a $250 prize, I could pay somebody to babysit the boys once in a while. Maybe, just maybe, if Grandpa heard that I won the STEM fair, he'd start to understand that Toivo and the boys and me are doing just fine here.

Well, *almost* fine. I haven't told Toivo about Alexi's teacher, and I haven't given him the note she said she put in his backpack.

Toivo calls over his shoulder, "Boys, you better listen to your sister, or I'm gonna get you!" He says it in a lighthearted way, which tells the boys he's being playful. But I know what he's got on his mind besides finding a job and proving to the court that he's a fit father.

Tomorrow is the anniversary of Mom and Matti's accident.

I wonder if we all feel it. If even the boys instinctively know that tomorrow is the day and that's why they're acting up even more than usual.

"I'm not in the mood, guys," I say to my brothers. "You better sit down right now and do your homework before I get mad."

I'd like to yell at them and tell them that if they don't shape up, we're all going to be taken away like Mark-Richard and Gary and have to live with Grandpa. But I don't.

"I'll make you a beechnut butter sandwich if you do your homework," I bribe them.

"With honey?" asks Alexi.

"Sure." Making beechnut butter is easy, but it takes a lot of time. I know that if I make the butter, I won't have time to get started on a STEM fair project.

"Beechnut butter!" says Toivo. "I haven't had that in ages. I'll take one, too, Fernny." He returns to his job hunting on the computer.

I just decide that I'll get up extra early and work on my project in the morning. I always like the mornings anyway.

Toivo and the boys sit piled in a recliner in front of the TV. They shovel piece after piece of beechnut butter sandwiches into their mouths. Their evening show is interrupted with a news brief. A reporter, standing in front of our school, checks her earpiece. "Am I on?" she asks the camera. Her face hardens and she says, "A Colter teacher has filed a petition to stop further development by Kloche's Hydraulic Fracturing Company.

Beechnut Butter

Shell the beechnuts. This takes a lot of time.
But the time is worth it. Turn on the oven to
350 degrees. Put the nuts in a single layer on
a baking sheet. Roast in the hot oven for about
10 minutes. Remove the pan. Once it and the
nuts cool down, rub the papery film off the
nuts. If you don't, the butter has an "off" taste.
Then toss all the nuts into a blender. Put in a
sprinkle of salt and about a capful of vegetable
oil. Blend on high until nice and smooth. Spoon
into a jar and cover tightly. Refrigerate. Spread
on bread and drizzle with honey. Maybe a little
cinnamon, too.

In the petition, Mr. Marcus Flores claims that Kloche's fracking company has a history of environmental violations across the state and destroys natural resources, pollutes groundwater, and causes irreparable damage to the environment. About his petition, Mr. Flores, had this to say..."

Mr. Flores appears on the television.

"Turn it up!" I shout. "That's my science teacher!"

Mikko punches the volume on the remote control.

"Fracking will level the last stand of old-growth pine left in this state and ruin the habitat of animals and plants," says Mr. Flores. "Fracking is known to pollute drinking water and is even suspected of causing earthquakes. We need to prohibit Kloche's from further development until the truth about fracking's effects can be revealed to Colter."

Then the camera cuts to a woman in a gray suit. She looks like a lawyer. The reporter asks her to respond.

"The fracking industry provides hundreds of high-paying jobs and rejuvenates communities. Kloche's is committed to providing affordable energy and a safe and clean environment. Thank you."

The reporter comes on again. "One thing's for sure,

Ed. This fight over fracking in the small town of Colter is not over yet. Back to you."

Toivo pops the boys off his lap. They fall onto the floor and immediately begin wrestling.

"Very sneaky," he says. He goes to the window and looks out at all the trees. "Why weren't there town meetings or news articles about it? Did they mean to sneak in here and get fracking before anyone could protest?"

"Can they do that?" I ask. "Come and frack wherever they want to? Are they going to destroy our grove?"

"Looks like it." He scruffs up my hair. "Well, it's not our grove, you know. Most of it belongs to Millner." Toivo chews on the side of his fingernail. "He doesn't mind that you're out there, I don't think. If he did, he'd have said something by now." He goes to the refrigerator and pulls out a beer.

"Millner's a murderer," I say.

Toivo pops the tab, and beer foam bubbles out and down the side of the can and onto the floor. He takes a long drink. His Adam's apple bobs up and down, three, four times.

"I don't want to talk about that much." His eyes get watery. I don't know if it's from the carbonation or from thinking about Mom and Matti. Then he points at me with the beer. "But don't be too hard on Millner."

On the day they died, Mom was driving into town to drop off Baby Matti at daycare and go into work to catch up on some grading. Horace Millner, coming from the other direction, fell asleep at the wheel. He'd just gotten off a fourteen-hour shift at one of Grandpa's factories, where he worked. He crossed the center line. Mom swerved, lost control, and flipped the car.

Grandpa fired Horace Millner.

Toivo was beside himself. But he never blamed Millner.

"Will Millner sell?" I ask. "Will he let the trees be cut down?"

Toivo adjusts the hearing aid in his ear. "Will he sell, did you say?" He doesn't wait for me to respond. "I don't know." He sets down his beer can, already empty, and picks at a blister on the palm of his hand. "I don't think so. But he might not have a choice. The county can annex that land to allow Kloche's to frack it if they want to."

"They can't!" I shout.

"They can," he says. "I've seen corporations convince governments to do lots of crazy things."

"Like what?"

A lone coyote howls. The boys jump up and race to the door to catch a look at the animal.

"*Hold* it!" Toivo shouts at them. "Never mind," he says to me. "I don't want to talk about it."

"But—"

"Bath time!" Toivo calls to the boys.

Both boys growl in pain, but it sounds like they're faking it.

"That's enough!" Toivo shouts, like he's really mad. But then he opens his eyes real wide, starts making snarling noises, and lifts his hands into claws. He dives down to the floor with the boys, playfully wrestling them.

He pretends to chew their necks and eat their feet. "I am a hungry coyote!" He tickles them and rubs a knuckle back and forth over their heads. They shriek with glee.

I stand above all of them with my hands on my hips. "You boys need to stop that this instant. You have to take a bath!"

"Rarrr!" Toivo growls, and swipes at my legs, so I decide to jump on top of all of them and grapple, too.

Cleaning up and job searching will have to wait.

When Toivo gets winded, we stop wrestling, and he gives each boy a soft smack on the bottom. "Go brush your fangs and take a bath, and I'll put on *Charlie Brown* for us to watch."

Toivo feels around on the floor for his hearing aid, which fell out in the skirmish, and pops it back in his ear. He heads to the fridge and fishes out another beer, and I follow him.

"What can we do about the woods?" I ask, determined to continue our earlier conversation. "I mean, what would we do without it? Lots of our food comes from out there. And where will the animals go?"

"I know it." He yawns and stretches. "But some of those fracking jobs pay pretty good, I imagine," he says.

"Who cares?" I wonder if Alkomso saw the news, and what she thinks about her dad's new job.

"Well, if getting a job with Kloche's was the one way I could convince the stupid court that I should keep you and your brothers, wouldn't that be worth it for us?" He doesn't wait for me to answer. He sits down at the computer and opens a search engine. He types in "Kloche Hydraulic Fracturing + jobs." Then he's clicking and scrolling and scrolling and clicking while I start the dishes.

I clank all the milk glasses into the soapy water, rinse them off, and toss them on the drying rack.

Toivo miraculously hears my racket and turns around to give me a stern grimace.

"Yeah," I begin, "but what about the trees?"

He puts his back to me again.

The more I think about it, the madder I get. I don't want fracking near my house. I don't want a wastewater pond taking over my woods.

He doesn't hear me. Or if he does hear me, he doesn't show it.

Next, I swipe all the plates into the sink at the same time. A big swoosh of suds spills over the sink and splashes onto the floor.

Again, Toivo turns around.

"Or the coyote? Or the bears? Or the birds?" I ask him "Where would they go?"

"What?"

"The birds." I articulate each word slowly. "Where would they go?"

He exhales. "Fern, I'm not saying I'm for fracking, but maybe we all have to think about how we live our lives," he says in a staccato delivery I'm not used to.

This time, I turn my back to him and scrub the pots and pans. He keeps talking, going on about how fracking for natural gas might be better than drilling for fossil fuels and junk I don't care about right now.

"That war they sent me to wasn't really about much more than oil. I could see that with my own eyes. I lost my dang hearing in one ear for it."

I don't know how he's making connections in his head. I've noticed that adults sometimes do this thing where they don't answer the question a kid has asked and instead start going on about something they're comfortable talking about instead.

He's still talking when I decide to interrupt him. "Yeah, but what about Mom?"

"What?" he says. "What do you mean, 'What about Mom?'"

"*Mom!*" I yell at him. "Those are her woods!"

Then, out of nowhere, Mikko dashes in with a toothpaste ring around his lips and his toothbrush hanging out of the corner of his mouth.

"Fern cut a duck off Millner's dog today," he says, spitting sudsy saliva. "She *did*!"

"Mikko!" I shout. I flick soapy water at his face.

Toivo spins around on his chair. "Oh, Fern, did you do that?" He shakes his head. "Millner has a right to teach his dogs not to kill his ducks."

I scoff. "Ranger didn't do it on purpose." I wipe my hands dry on a dish towel and then slap the cloth onto the counter.

"Ranger?" says Toivo. "Who's Ranger?" He opens his eyes wide with understanding. "You named one of Millner's dogs? Fernny, those aren't your dogs."

"Millner doesn't deserve him. He doesn't deserve those woods, and he doesn't deserve Ranger! He deserves to be sad, sad, *sad*."

Toivo sighs. "I think you've had a long day. Maybe you better go to bed." His chin is tucked tight into his neck.

"I'm *not* tired," I state. I lift my chin up. "Mom loved those woods! Millner killed her and Matti, so the least he could do is not sell the woods!" I eyeball Toivo.

We stare at each other this way for a few seconds.

I'm tall and confident as a pine tree, ready to counter whatever he comes up with next.

But instead of fighting, he relaxes his shoulders, his arms, and his face and looks away from me. "I get it," he says to the wall.

Sometimes the despair is so crushing that I wish that Toivo, Alexi, Mikko, and me had all been in the car when sleeping Millner in his pickup truck crossed the dotted yellow line on an early-morning two-laner in the middle of nowhere just as my mom happened to be on the road with my sleeping baby brother tucked tight in his car seat. I sometimes think it would have been better if we had all gone together.

I am not a crier. But right now in the back of my head, a force builds like a broken dam of rushing misery. My eyes wet with the pressure.

Toivo moves toward me. He grabs me with his right arm and presses me tight against his chest. He holds me there for a minute, and he hiccups trying to control his own sobbing. Him being close to crying makes me want to cry. I hold my breath to prevent it.

Once he steadies, he says into the top of my head, "I think Millner is about the saddest soul I ever knew."

He squeezes me until I have to exhale. "He didn't do it on purpose, either."

When I finally compose myself, he says, "One of these days, you're going to have to cut the duck from Millner's neck, too."

Chapter 9

On the anniversary of Mom's death, I wake with a start. The trucks aren't running. I wonder what woke me. Then I hear *rat-a-tat-tat-tat. Rat-a-tat-tat-tat.*

I get up and go the window. It's snowing great big clumps. The whole world seems tamped down with weight.

Rat-a-tat-tat-tat.

A few inches to my right, outside the window, is a huge downy woodpecker clinging to the side of the house. Mom's favorite bird. He's white and black with a red breast. His beady eye seems to be looking right at me. I rap on the window glass. *Rap-a-rap-rap-rap.*

The woodpecker stiffens. I hold my breath.

Then his head drills into the wall. *Rat-a-tat-tat-tat-tat*.

I smile. It's almost like Mom has sent me a gift.

I watch him for a while, until I decide to get dressed and head downstairs.

I know that Toivo will probably stay in bed all day. Last night he sat up in the old reclining chair with Mikko and Alexi on his lap, watching *A Charlie Brown Thanksgiving* until all three fell asleep. I half carried and half walked the boys to bed about midnight. I shook Toivo, but he wouldn't budge. Thirteen empty beer cans lay on the carpet. I went to bed, and I didn't hear when he woke up and moved to his room.

His room, which used to be Mom's room, too, is just off the kitchen. He left the door ajar. Now I can see his feet, still in boots, hanging over the end of the bed. He's facedown, and he's snoring softly. Baby Matti's crib is exactly where it was when he was alive, off Mom's side of the bed. I stand for a minute and look in.

It's easy to remember Mom there, too. Sometimes in the mornings, I'd come down and see her lying sideways, nursing the baby. She'd whisper, *Good morning, Fernny*, and point at the baby and then put her finger to her lips to remind me to be quiet. I'd come in and kiss her and rub Matti's bald head. He didn't have a lick of hair, but he was still cute. In those days, Toivo was already out the door, up before dawn, shoveling snow or off to work by the time I woke up.

Toivo stirs a little bit, as though he's having a nightmare. I step back and let him work it out with some privacy.

I quietly collect all the cans in a garbage bag and put them in the recycling bin. I don't want to wake anyone. I look around for what to make for breakfast. The cereal is all gone. There's only enough oatmeal for one bowl.

When Mom was alive, we kept hens out back in a coop. So we always had fresh eggs. Lots of them. Mom had a way with birds. The chickens followed her around. And she could call in cardinals and blue jays by imitating their calls.

After she died, we butchered the chickens. And the cardinals and blue jays stopped coming around so often.

I pull out the flour and salt from the cupboard and then the yeast from the refrigerator. I'll make bread. It's easy. I dump four cups or so of flour in a big bowl and fluff it up with a fork. Then I tap in some salt. I fluff it some more. Scoop a little yeast into a bowl. Add water. Just as I turn on the tap to get the water, I feel a hand on my shoulder and a kiss on the top of my head.

"Mornin'," Toivo says. He's wearing the same clothes as yesterday—an old pair of jeans and a blue work shirt from a job he used to have. "Sorry about the mess."

I let the water run until it's warm. I hold a bowl under to collect about two cups.

"What are you doing up?" I shut off the water. "I thought you'd stay in bed."

Toivo pinches sleep from the corners of his eyes. "Yeah," he says real slow and quiet. He stares out the window, where the snow falls in giant flakes.

I'm worried I said the wrong thing. "I mean," I begin, "it's okay if you stay in bed. I'm taking the boys to Alkomso's today so we can work on our STEM projects."

"STEM project? What's yours? Do you need help?"

I do need help, but I don't feel like it's the right time to ask for it. "I'm not sure yet," I say. "But I'll figure it out."

"Yeah," he says again. "I'm sure you will." He opens the cupboard. He takes a gulp from his bottle of medicine, grimaces, and shakes his head. "I hate this day," he says as he slips on his work boots without tying them and steps outside. Soon I smell cigarette smoke wafting up through the crack between the floor and door.

I pour the water and yeast into the flour and salt. I stir until it's all one big ball. *Don't do too much mixing*, I hear Mom say. *Incorporate everything and then leave the dough alone. It knows what to do without you.* I cover and set it on top of the stove to rise.

The door opens and Toivo shakes off the snow that's collected on his head and shoulders. He sets a load of chopped wood on the floor and huffs. "Better get that woodstove burning. I'm going to head out to the woods. Saw some partridge tracks out there the other day. The birds will be easy to find today."

I sit at the table beneath the kitchen window. Cold air wafts in through a crack, created when Mikko threw Alexi's hockey skate at his head and missed. Papers and bills make an unwieldy pile on the table. Lots of the bills say FINAL NOTICE or URGENT, and some of the unopened letters have fallen in the space between the table and the wall. I flip through the stack, find another letter from the Children's Protective Services lady,

Mom's Bread

Dissolve a spoonful of yeast in a teacup of warm water until it's nice and creamy. In a big bowl, mix five cups of flour, a spoonful of salt, and a spoonful of sugar. Set aside. Add the yeasty mixture to another cup of warm water. Stir it up. Dump it into the flour mixture. Mix just until the dough forms a ball. Not too much! Cover with an old newspaper page and let rise. Heat oven and bread pan to 450 degrees. Carefully transfer bread dough to hot pan. Bake 30 minutes.

Miss Tassel. The letter says she'll be out for a home inspection and inventory in a week.

That means we'll have to get the house cleaned.

At least if we had a dog, he could eat all the food that falls on the floor and kill the mice that hide behind the refrigerator and climb all over the counter at night, leaving their little chew marks in the butter.

The ceiling rumbles, rattling the glass light fixture above my head as Mikko and Alexi tumble out of the bed they share.

"Me first!" I hear one of them say upstairs.

"No, me!" says the other. They stumble down the stairs, elbowing each other out of the way, asking me what's to eat.

"I'm baking bread," I tell them. "We'll have toast and jam in a while."

"I just want jam," says Mikko. "I don't need bread."

"I don't think so, mister," I say.

Mom and I made the jam. We still have four pints left from her last batch.

Maybe this summer I'll make it just like she did.

I turn on the TV to a morning cartoon. The house is noisy and warm and almost feels normal. I tidy up a bit, and then I watch TV with the boys until the bread

Plum-and-Currant Jam

In July, collect an ice-cream pail of red currants. They grow wild on short bushes with the maple-shaped leaves about 50 paces into the woods from the gravel road. Don't be discouraged by their disagreeable smell. Put the top on the ice cream pail and put the currants in the freezer. In early August, pick the wild plums from the giant bush on the northern edge of the woods. In the biggest pot you've got, slowly cook down 4 cups of plums and 4 cups of currants. Turn the fruits up to boiling, then turn down to low-medium heat and simmer until there's mostly liquid with some pulp. Slowly add 8 cups of sugar. Stir constantly. Ladle into clean and heated jars. Seal.

is done. When the timer dings, I cut slices and slather each one with plum-and-currant jam.

Mikko licks the jam off four slices of bread, and when he thinks I'm not looking, he slips the soggy bread between the couch cushions.

"Hey," I say firmly. "No way."

Alexi eats three slices but sets the crust on the arm of the couch.

"Pick that up," I say. "Throw it in the sink, at least. Quit acting like gross little pigs."

"Oink," says Alexi.

"Oink, oink," says Mikko.

After they eat, I put the dishes in the sink and dry the laundry. Toivo's cell phone rings several times. Each time it's an 800 number, probably a debt collector. I tell the boys to get their snow pants and boots on, and they do.

Mikko's got on two different boots, and Alexi wears Toivo's socks on his hands for mittens, but I don't care. "Let's go," I tell them. "Maybe we'll see Ranger."

"I want a dog so bad I could scream," says Mikko. He clenches his fists and baps them around as though he's playing drums.

"I want a dog so sore I could pee," says Alexi.

When I'm in charge of the boys, I try to remember all the things Mom used to say to them. They scrapped a lot when she was alive, too. "We're going to Alkomso's and are going to try and have a nice time."

"Yeah," says Mikko. "Don't ruin it."

We mosey on toward Colter. It's a small town with hardly any stores open and nothing to do if you don't know how to entertain yourself, which most kids don't. The boys break twigs off of the trees and scrape them along the slushy snow that's building up. It's early for snow, even for Colter. The boys and I walk faster than usual to keep warm.

I decide to take a detour. "Follow me, guys. Let's say hi to Mom."

I lead the boys behind the small church and through a little gate into the cemetery. Our mom is buried right next to her mom, who died of breast cancer when Mom was just a little girl.

I kneel down and try to feel Mom's presence. It occurs to me that if the grove gets cut down, this will be the only place I might be able to feel near to her. The boys sit down, crisscross applesauce right in the wet snow. Mikko stares at the headstone as though he's trying to figure out the words.

We didn't care whether Mom had a headstone or not, but Grandpa did. Without consulting us, he had a big, shiny black one made. It reads JOHANNA, BELOVED DAUGHTER AND MOTHER. Skipping WIFE and skipping her married name were Grandpa's ways of sticking it to Toivo. Toivo won't come out here anymore.

The boys pick at the crisp, dry grass poking up through the snow, and I sweep the flakes away from Mom's marker. We just sit there in silence for a while.

"Children," a deep voice says.

My blood goes ice-cold. The boys jump.

Grandpa.

Mikko and Alexi stand up and wipe off their snow pants. I stand up, too, and pull the boys close to me.

But they lunge away from me and hug Grandpa's legs.

"Hi, Grandpa!" they squeal. Grandpa lifts both of them up at the same time and kisses them and bear-hugs them. His clothes get all wet from the snow on the boys, but Grandpa doesn't care. He squishes them right up to his face. Then he reaches out and pulls me into his huge body and embraces me strongly.

"Fern, you've got the most beautiful hair in the world," he says, setting the boys down. "Look at that.

It's slick and rich as oil." He takes off his cowboy hat and fluffs his thick hair. "Same color as mine!"

"Yep," I say. "It is the same. But it's only hair."

"You do remind me of your mother, Fern. You are a lucky girl." He pulls up his pants by the belt buckle that says BIG JOHN.

"Did you bring us something, Grandpa?" The boys spin around him and dig their hands into Grandpa's coat pockets. Alexi pulls out a money clip. Grandpa takes it out of his hands and peels off three twenties. I want to scold the boys and tell them we don't take handouts, but it's too late. After handing one to each of the boys, Grandpa stretches one toward me.

A twenty. I could buy bread, milk, eggs, butter, and flour with that.

I look away. "No thanks."

"I thought you might say that." He refolds it and puts the clip back in his pocket. Mikko and Alexi take off running through the headstones.

The boys don't really understand what's happening between Toivo and Grandpa. All they know of Grandpa is candy, toys, and trips to the zoo or the amusement park. The boys see Grandpa and immediately start thinking about his lake mansion-cabin with enough separate bedrooms and bathrooms for everyone, and a maid who cleans up. To them, Grandpa means fun boat rides and fishing poles and fireworks. But now I'm old enough to understand his ways.

The way he bad-mouths Toivo whenever he talks to us.

The way he buys us toys we can only use at his place.

The way he tries to break up what's left of my family.

"We gotta get going, Grandpa," I say. "It was nice to see you."

"I didn't mean to chase you away. If you want to stay with your mom for a while longer, please do. I won't bother you."

I don't feel like Mom is here anyway. Even though this is technically where she is, the space isn't warm or comforting in the way that the woods are. Being here on the anniversary of her death just feels like a responsibility. An expectation.

"We're meeting some friends," I tell Grandpa. "Got some schoolwork to do."

"That's good to hear. Are you keeping up? In school?"

"Pretty much," I say.

He eyes me sharply, as though he doesn't believe what I'm saying. He jingles keys in his pocket. "How's your STEM project coming along? My company donated a nice prize, you know."

"Yeah, Grandpa. You told me that already."

"You know, Fern, all this stuff with Toivo—I'm just doing what's best for you and the boys. I can't have you kids flunking grades. Your mom would not want that."

I shift my feet and cross my arms. He's right about Mom.

"He's just not fit," Grandpa goes on. "He can't even take care of himself. You have to trust me on this. I know best."

I uncross my arms and wave the boys toward me. "We have to go now," I say. "Boys! Let's go!"

They come flying, jump into Grandpa's arms, and kiss him good-bye.

"See you, Grandpa," I say.

"Hold on there," he snaps. His giant hand squeezes my shoulder. He tugs me into a hug. He's warm and smells like tobacco and leather. "You kids need me," he says. "And I need you."

At first I resist. I keep my arms and back stiff. But Grandpa just holds on and on and won't let me go.

Finally, I give in and soften up into his big belly. Being hugged by Grandpa feels kind of safe. But then I worry that I'm betraying Toivo, so I let go.

"Okay, Grandpa," I say. "We have to go. Bye."

After we've walked on some, I turn around and see Grandpa down on one knee in front of Mom's grave with his hat in his hand.

Chapter 10

When we get to Alkomso's apartment, I punch in the security code and climb the stairs. Two of her little sisters swing the door open, grab my arm, and screech, "Come in! Get in here!"

The house smells of roasted goat and almond milk and garlic. Sometimes I think Alkomso's home smells weird, but she thinks my house smells weird, too. Like feet, she says.

"Hullo," yells Alkomso's mother from the kitchen of the small apartment. She says something to the little girls in Somali that makes them back up and pout.

Abdisalom pops out from behind a couch, and my little brothers are off like hounds after a rabbit.

"Hi, Hamdi!" I say. That's Alkomso's mother's name.

Alkomso waves a notebook at me. "Did you see Mr. Flores on TV last night? I started a story about a science teacher who hates fracking and a lady lawyer who represents Kloche's. They fall in love. It's very tragic and very romantic."

Hamdi raises the spatula she's using for cooking. "You stop thinking about boys all the time, and put that story away! Get to work on the STEM project!"

The baby, Kaltumo, wails in a bassinet Hamdi has placed in the kitchen, where she's cooking. I lean over and grab the baby's tiny fist. I stroke her hand.

"What's the matter with her?" I ask Hamdi.

"I don't know. All she does is cry." Hamdi doesn't appear nervous or worried. She simply pats the baby's belly and coos something else I don't understand. The baby smiles, but then, as soon as Hamdi returns to her kitchen work, starts crying again.

"I'll hold her," I offer.

Hamdi waves her hand. "Sure, sure. You hold her."

I lift Kaltumo to my chest. She immediately stops

crying and reaches for my lips. I put my nose to her hair and sniff. I love the scent of babies: curdled milk and baby powder. Matti smelled just this way. My eyes well up. I give Kaltumo a kiss on the cheek and lay her back in the bassinet and give her the edge of her blanket to hold. She puts it to her mouth and starts sucking.

Alkomso sets up a laptop on a card table.

"Where did you get this computer?" I ask.

"The library!" she says. "You can borrow all kinds of technology from there." Sometimes I don't know why I don't think about things like that. Alkomso's family doesn't have much money, either, but they always seem to be able to outsmart being poor.

She clicks around and opens up a document called "What Is Fracking?" She says, "My project is *so* confusing. Lots of people think fracking is good because it brings jobs, but there are lots and lots of people who say that it poisons the air and water."

"I wonder why Mr. Flores didn't tell us what he really thought about fracking," I say.

"Too political!" Hamdi shouts from the kitchen.

"Quit eavesdropping, Mom!" Alkomso scolds. Then she leans close to me. "Mom said that Mr. Flores is in big trouble with the school board already. She said that Mrs. Peterson is working overtime to get him fired."

I pull on a strand of my hair. "That would be terrible. He's the best science teacher ever."

"I know," says Alkomso. "What's your project? Have you decided? If you haven't, you can be my partner."

"No," I snap.

She tilts her head.

"I mean..." I take a breath. "I mean, thanks for offering, but I'll figure out my own project."

"Are you still mad at me about what I said in class?"

"No. I'm not mad about that. I just...I just think that if I do my own project and get a good score, maybe Grandpa will leave Toivo and us alone."

"Your grandpa just needs to give it up. Maybe he should get a girlfriend and think about something else."

I laugh. And I feel relieved. I don't want to have a fight with Alkomso. Especially now that Mark-Richard is gone and I'm not sure when he'll be back. I don't want to lose another friend.

When Alkomso and her family first came to Colter, I wasn't her friend. I can still picture her on her first day at our school. I can still see her brown eyes scanning the classroom. She checked each face for a hint of a friend.

When she looked at me, I met her hope with a stony glare. Those were the days when I was trying hard to fit in with Margot and her friends. I was one of the girls who used to snicker about Alkomso's clothes, especially her scarves. I was one of the girls who used to pretend she had "germs."

At recess time, I would sit under the big tree with Margot and the rest. We'd scoff at Maura's socks. We'd laugh about the hair on Bernice's arms. We'd say Letitia had lice. We made fun of everyone for anything.

I never felt safe around them. Every morning my stomach roiled. My forehead singed. I would lie on my pillow and feel behind my ear, where I knew my hair was changing. The gray hairs grew stiff and wiry. Every morning I wondered if this would be the day Margot would notice.

One day I was surprised to see Mom waiting for me outside my classroom door after school with Hamdi, who was waiting for Alkomso. One of my so-called friends elbowed me and said, "Look at that old lady with a new baby. Gross!" Because after Mom had

Matti, her tummy hung over her jeans like a mushroom cap, and she didn't color her hair, so most of her head was silver.

I walked right past my mom and pretended she wasn't mine. Mom watched me, understanding exactly what I was doing.

I didn't really like myself for a long time after that.

I didn't like saying nasty things about the other girls. I didn't like talking about cute boys all the time. I didn't really have the slightest interest in jewelry or nail art. I always knew that if I made one mistake, Margot and her friends would turn on me.

Which they did.

About a month after Mom and Matti died, the girls stopped talking to me. I would try to sit with them beneath the tree, and they would purposefully create a circle with their knees and not let me in it.

They would pretend they couldn't see or hear me.

They would say things like, "I understand her mom died, but now she's just trying to get attention."

And "She must like that her mom died, because now all the teachers give her extra time to get her homework done."

And "She doesn't have to pretend to be so sad about her little brother. He was just a baby. She hardly had time to even know him."

What's really embarrassing is that I was still frantic to be their friend, and so I kept trying. I think I was scared of any more change.

Then one day, during reading class, Alkomso helped me out. I had lost my reading book. I just sat there when the teacher said to get it out. Alkomso scraped her whole desk and then her chair right next to mine. It was super noisy, but she didn't care. Then she pulled out her reading book, set it on the crack between our desks, and opened it.

When Mom died, Alkomso became the kind of friend to me that I should have been to her.

I'm embarrassed about all that now. I can't take it back, but I wish I could.

I flip through a few pages of her book while the little kids throw pillows at one another.

"The drawings in here make fracking look very neat and orderly," I say.

"I know! Look at all the green grass around the drills. And all the shiny trucks and hard hats."

"Yeah." I nod. "Um, do you think it *really* looks like that?"

She leans over my shoulders and stares down at a drawing with a pond labeled WASTEWATER. It's shiny and blue. "Yeah," she says. "Why not?"

"I don't know," I say. All the kids in the apartment are making a racket.

"Quiet down!" Hamdi says. "Kaltumo needs her nap."

I slap the book shut. "Let's take the boys for a walk. Get them out of your mom's way for a while."

"Yeah," Alkomso agrees.

I whisper, "Maybe we can go see where those trucks are going, do some research for your project."

She nods.

Hamdi would have a heart attack if she knew we were taking the boys out that far, so we just tell her and the boys we're going sledding.

Once we get outside, Mikko kicks snow on Alexi and Abdisalom. They get mad and yell and carry on like a bunch of hooligans.

As we're walking past the American Legion bar, I notice an old Dodge truck, two-tone white and blue, with a crooked snowplow attached to the front. On the bumper there's a sticker that reads No Fracking!

That's definitely Horace Millner's old truck, the one that drove Mom and Matti upside down into the ditch. But the sticker is brand-new.

It's confusing, knowing that Millner and I are on the same side.

I slow way down and try to see through the dark windows. At first all I can see are the neon lights of beer signs. But then I fix my gaze on a man hunched over a coffee cup at the end of the bar. He's all alone.

"What are you looking at?" Alkomso asks.

"Nothing. I'm not looking at anything."

She steps up to the window and presses her nose against it. "Who is that?"

"No one," I say.

"Is that him? The one who—"

I tug her arm. "Let's go."

She walks along beside me. My head spins with thoughts. Does the sticker mean that Millner isn't going to sell his land? But even if he doesn't, Toivo said the county can simply take it if they want to. I've never seen Millner's truck at the bar before. Is he thinking today about what he did to my mom and brother? Is he going to drink his guilt away? But I didn't see a bottle or glass of beer.

"Looked like he was just drinking coffee, right?" I ask Alkomso.

She nods.

"Sometimes I used to wonder about how he dealt with it," I say. I kick a stone out ahead of me. "Not that I feel sorry for him or anything. But I wondered if he drank a lot or something." I almost add *like Toivo*, but I don't.

"Adults do all kinds of dumb things to handle problems. But drinking coffee doesn't seem like a dumb way to do it." She stuffs her hands in her pockets. "My mom sneaks cigarettes. Don't tell my dad!"

My mouth forms a big O. "Wow, I had no idea."

"Adults can be sneaky," she adds. "Very sneaky."

The boys push and shove one another out ahead of us.

"Move it, fatty," Abdisalom says to Alkomso.

She points back at the apartment. "You do that again, and you are going home! Got it?" Abdisalom giggles but nods.

"Move it, fatty," Alexi says to me.

I glare at him. I feel a little sorry for myself. It's a tough-enough day the way it is, without my annoying little brothers. I wish Toivo had offered to take them partridge hunting with him. I understand the need to be alone, especially out in the wild, especially on a day like today. But I could use a break, too.

Chapter 11

I lead our caravan out of town and down the dirt road, which is slippery and uneven. The mud sucks at our boots. Alkomso holds her skirt high. Even so, it's heavy in the back with the weight of muck.

For a long while, no one complains. The snow has stopped, clouds have moved east, the sun's out, with sun dogs on either side of it, and the temperature is climbing, melting the snow that's already fallen.

The boys dart back and forth between the road and the woods. They hurl snowballs at one another and swing at them with sticks. The little white bombs explode. Snowy shrapnel lands in my hair. They swipe at one another with the sleds.

We all stop at Mark-Richard's and stare down the driveway. The snow has completely covered everything, so that it's hard to tell his house was ever there.

"*Gary!*" shouts Alexi. "Gary, are you there?"

"He's not, dummy," says Mikko. "He's in a foster home."

"Well, when is he coming back?" Alexi asks.

"To where, you idiot?" says Mikko. "His house is gone! You think he's going to live in a snow fort or what?"

"Knock it off, Mikko," I say. "He doesn't know any better." I put my hand on Alexi's head. "I don't know when he's coming back."

"That's *bull*!" Alexi kicks me in the leg and runs off. "Ow!"

Mikko and Abdisalom chase him. Pretty soon they're playing and searching for bear tracks. When the boys describe their encounter with the bear, Abdisalom's eyes widen and dart back and forth.

"Don't worry," says Alexi. "That dog who kills ducks will come and protect us. He's a SuperDog, and Fernny named him SuperRanger."

Alkomso and I stare at Mark-Richard's old place for a while longer. Near the woodpile, I see a neat stack of branches. I remember what Mark-Richard told me about having to find more firewood for winter. Looks like he collected those branches before the fire. For some reason, it makes my heart hurt.

When we pass our house, I notice that Toivo's truck is gone. I wonder where he went. Usually when he hunts, he simply walks out into Millner's woods.

"Fern," Alkomso finally says, "how much farther to the fracking site, do you think?"

"It's just a little ways yet, I think," I tell her. Alexi packs a snowball and heaves it at me. It smacks me right in the head. I claw a wet mass of slush out of my hair, and Alkomso wipes a snow glob off my shoulder.

We hear the grumble of a struggling diesel engine coming up behind us.

"Come on," Alkomso says. "Get into the ditch, Abdisalom."

Alexi scrapes the tip of his boot into a rut in the road. He's creating a little pool.

"You, too, Alexi," I say. "Come on. Get off the road."

"Just a *minute*!" he shouts. I grab the collar of his coat and drag him out of the way.

We wait. The first thing I notice is the crooked snowplow. As the pickup gets closer, my head gets hotter and hotter.

"It's Millner," I whisper. "Don't look at him!"

"Why not?" asks Alkomso.

"I don't know. J-just don't!" I stutter.

Alkomso turns herself then the boys by telling them she thinks she saw a moose out in the woods.

"There aren't any moose around here," Mikko says.

"Well," she says, "I don't know. Maybe it was the bear." She pushes them in the direction of the woods. "Let's go see!"

"Maybe we can find a big pile of bear poop!" says Abdisalom.

The boys make binoculars out of their hands and fingers and peer into the grove. Then they kick through the snow and toward the trees.

Millner slows down. His engine chugs and chugs like it might die, but it doesn't. As he passes by, he leans over and gets a good look at me.

I stand still.

He drives on ahead a little ways, brakes with a squeak, and stops. The reverse lights on his truck go on as he backs toward me.

My head is hot. Maybe he's going to try and hit me with his truck. Maybe he wants to kill me, too.

His wheels pass about a foot in front of my feet.

I can't move.

Millner leans over across his bench seat. He rolls down the window, releasing the smells of chewing tobacco and leather and dust.

"Ah," he begins. "You kids," he says. His voice is barely above a whisper. He sounds old, like a grandpa. I wonder for the first time if Horace Millner has a family.

He blinks and studies my face for a moment, then puts his hand on the shifter and puts the pickup back into first gear.

"You kids," he says again. "Watch out for them big trucks. They drive too fast. Don't look where they're going."

I say nothing. My whole head is burning up.

He concentrates on what to say next. "Ah," he starts, "you're Toivo's girl, ain't you." He doesn't pose it as a question. He says the words as though he knows the answer.

I nod.

"Yeah." He looks over my shoulder toward where Alkomso, Abdisalom, Mikko, and Alexi are, raises a crooked finger and points. "And them two. They're Toivo's other little boys."

I nod again.

"Good man, that Toivo." He waves his finger out the window. "There's poison ivy. Between the pines."

I stare down the road, not at him and not at where he's gesturing.

"There's jewelweed out there, too. Works good for the rash." He swallows.

"I already know that" is all I can say.

"Yeah. I'm sure you do." He lifts his foot from the clutch, and the truck inches forward a bit. Even as the pickup moves, he says, "You the one who cut the duck from my dog?"

I shrug one shoulder.

"Yeah," he says. "I thought so." He steps on the gas and drives away.

As he approaches his driveway about a quarter mile down, I say it. "You killed my mom. You killed my brother."

Of course, he can't hear me. But somehow, saying the words and letting them float on the air feels like enough.

The noise of Millner's truck arriving draws the

dogs. They run to greet him in a barking and howling swarm. As he drives out of sight down his long, narrow driveway, all the dogs follow but two—Ranger and a black Lab whose belly hangs low to the ground.

When I raise my hand and wave, Ranger barks a short blast that makes me jump. He runs toward us a ways, then stops to look back at the other dog. The black Lab wags her tail wildly until Ranger trots back to her. Side by side, they saunter down Horace Millner's driveway and disappear.

Alkomso comes up behind me. "I think those two dogs are in love." She links her arms around mine. "Are you okay?" she asks.

I shrug my shoulders. My heart beats a million times a minute. "I don't know."

When we find the boys, Abdisalom is on the ground with his bare hand buried in the snow. His face contorts in pain. His lips go tight. His eyes are clenched closed.

"We told him not to touch it!" Mikko says. He points to a small bush with gnarled red leaves and shriveled white berries. Poison ivy. In every season, every part of the poison ivy plant is toxic.

"Nu-uh," says Alexi, "Mikko dared him!"

"I did not," says Mikko.

Alkomso kneels next to Abdisalom. She grabs his wrist and pulls his hand out of the snow. "Sissy's going to fix it," she croons.

"No!" I tell her. "Don't touch his hand! The oil might still be on him."

She calmly lets go of his wrist. "All right, all right."

Abdisalom moans and kicks his legs. "Owie, it burns."

"Put your hand back in the snow," Alkomso says. "Right?" she asks me.

"Yes. Keep it in the snow for a minute."

I kick aside snow, sweeping at it in broad leg strokes until I discover a patch of jewelweed. The tallest leaves of one plant stick out above the snow. Water drops glisten on it like jewels. That's how the plant got its name. I pull it up and break the stem in half. A clear, sticky gel oozes from the plant.

I rush to Abdisalom. "Hold your hand up."

He does. A tiny blister is already beginning to form.

I rub the plant all over Abdisalom's hand. "Get me another one," I tell Mikko and Alexi. "And watch out for poison ivy."

"Duh," says Mikko.

Within a minute, they come back with jewelweed up to their noses. As I rub the plant gel on Abdisalom's hand, Alkomso distracts him by talking about the dogs, what's for dinner, and whatever else comes to her mind. Within five minutes, he's calm and smiling.

I apply the gel of two more plants until Abdisalom starts to protest, "I'm fine!" When I'm done, I stuff jewelweed leaves into his mitten.

"That stuff is amazing," Alkomso says to me. "Someone should write down all the wonderful things you can find for free out in the woods."

Someone *should* do that, I think, and I realize it's not the first time I've thought this.

Chapter 12

We walk another half mile. Pine trees, thirty and forty feet tall, reach toward the sky. Sometimes when one of us would catch a cold or get a chill, Mom would come out here, cut a branch from a low-hanging bough, and use the needles to make us a cup of pine-needle tea. She'd put the rest of the branch in a vase to keep the needles fresh. That way she could make another batch when she needed to. "Pine-needle tea is full of vitamin C," she would say. "And it'll clear your nose right up." I never minded getting sick, because it meant we could go out to the woods and get the needles.

In spring, the pine trees smelled like robin's eggs, ice melt, tadpoles, wild violets, and soaked pinecones. In summer, the pine trees smelled like cool shade and ferns. In autumn, the pine trees smelled like milkweed seed and drying bones. In winter, the pine trees smelled like hoar frost, oyster mushrooms, freshwater clams, and Christmas.

And whatever time of year it was, when Mom brought the boughs inside, the house smelled like all the good things outside.

As we continue on, suddenly the woods stop, as though the trees have simply been sheared from the land. It's a shocking difference. One step back and we are in the woods. Right here, we are at the end of the wild. The earth is covered with branches and dead pine needles, but the huge white pine grove that used to be here is leveled. On one end is what looks like a parking lot for the workers. There are two ruts in the dirt, where the workers must drive, leading from where we stand all the way to the lot.

Mikko turns around, confused, and then looks at me and says, "What the—"

Up ahead, there's a muddy earthen berm with an

orange snow fence at the top of it. Huge No Trespassing signs hang everywhere. Protective Headgear Required Past This Point, another sign reads.

"That must be the work area," I tell Alkomso. "This doesn't look exactly like the drawings from the book, does it?"

Alkomso doesn't answer. I go over to a kiosk that says Personnel Only Past This Point. A map behind a glass pane details the construction progress. On it, where Horace Millner's property is, a blue rectangle is labeled Proposed Wastewater Holding Pond.

"There it is. Right in Millner's woods."

"Yeah, I'll bet they offered him a lot of money for that land."

"That doesn't matter."

The boys come up for a look, too. Mikko sounds out a word. "P-ON-duh. Pond?" he asks. "That sounds great! We can swim in it!" Then he works out the rest of the words. "Wastewater?" he asks. "What's that?"

"Sounds like a toilet exploded!" shouts Alexi.

"Or dinosaur diarrhea," adds Abdisalom.

"Or frog turds," says Mikko.

While Alkomso and I look at the map, I notice an

electrical sound humming all around us, but I can't tell where it's coming from.

"Do you know what the wastewater is?" I ask. "Exactly?"

"I read about it," Alkomso says. She seems hesitant to tell me.

"And?"

"Um, water and sand."

"Anything else?"

"And maybe a few chemicals," she adds. "That's all I remember."

"Huh," I say. "Sounds...dirty."

She shrugs. "There are a lot of nice cars over in the parking lot. I bet the workers make a good living."

My face gets hot. "Maybe we should go and take a look inside the work area. You know...for your project."

"I don't think we're supposed to go in there," she says. "We'll probably get into trouble."

But I'm already walking, and the boys are following me. I don't look back, but I think Alkomso is following, too.

I approach the berm the company built. "Stay down here," I say to the boys.

I scramble up the dirt. Rocks and snow fall inside

my boot. The knees of my jeans get wet and dirty. Soon Alkomso, soppy and muddy, is right beside me.

When we get to the top, a variety of sounds become clear—the beeping of machinery as it backs up, the grinding of bulldozer tracks, the release of pressure from hydraulic pumps. We reach the fence and use our fingers to widen the small squares of the plastic. Then we align our eyeballs so that we can see inside.

There's a huge hole dug out of the earth and then smoothed over. Grandpa's piping is stacked neatly at one end of the hole.

"Oh!" says Alkomso. "It's like a little city!"

"All this used to be trees," I say. "I can't believe it."

Abdisalom is trying to get up the berm. "I want to see. I want to see. Help me up!"

Alexi and Mikko tackle the berm, too.

"I told you to stay down there," I say.

They don't listen. Alexi tries to pull Abdisalom up, but they both go sliding back down the rise. Mikko falls forward, at the top, at my feet. He crawls to the fence and looks through it.

"Holy cow!" he says. "What in the hell-o kitty happened to the woods?"

There is a strange scent on the breeze, something

that reminds me of when you crush an aspirin between two spoons. Alkomso puts the end of her scarf over her nose. The smell of pine is gone.

"It smells like poison now," I say.

A few feet beyond the inside of the fence, a shallow cavity begins, big as twenty acres or so. Some of the trucks we've been seeing on our road are lined up in one area. Some are driving in and out of the work site over makeshift roads. Near where we are standing lie basic building materials—sheet metal and ready-to-assemble ceiling and wall frames. Small trailers have been placed side by side. Outside one of the trailers, work shirts and jeans are drying on a sawhorse.

"Look over there," says Mikko. He pokes his finger through the fence and points to the center of the work site. There, workers walk on the metal beams of something that looks like the skeleton of a pyramid. "What's that going to be?"

"I don't know," I say.

"The drill," says Alkomso. "That's going to be the drill."

Then I see something on the other end of the pit, right inside the entrance gate.

Toivo's pickup.

I squint and scan the work site. *Where is he? What's he doing here?*

He said he was going partridge hunting.

A job. That's the only thing he could be doing here. Getting a job. I flip through my memories and try to remember exactly what he said. I thought we agreed that he would not work here. I thought he understood how I felt about it.

I take off my mittens and throw them on the ground. I grip the fence and shake it.

"Hey," says Alkomso. "What's wrong?"

"Toivo's in there." I point. "Getting a job."

"What?" She looks to where I'm looking. "Are you sure?"

"Why else would he be in there?"

She grabs my arm and pulls me to the ground. "Get down! There he is!"

Toivo steps out of a white trailer that says Office and walks across a bunch of boards thrown down as a path and gets into his truck. Another man steps out of the trailer with a clipboard. They wave at each other. Toivo drives toward the gate, which opens electronically to let him out. Alkomso and I stay on our bellies, watching his truck turn onto the gravel road, which leads back home. We don't move until his pickup is out of sight.

"He told me he was going hunting," I say.

"Maybe he meant hunting for a job."

"No, he didn't mean that."

"Maybe it wouldn't be so bad," she says. "My dad's going to work here."

"It's terrible, Alkomso. *Terrible!*"

"Why? People have to make a living, Fern. Maybe if Toivo got a job there, your grandpa wouldn't be trying to take you away. Maybe you could get a better house."

I can tell that Alkomso thinks she's being helpful, but her words make me so mad. "I can't believe you want these frackers to put a poison pond in my woods, and you want Toivo to work for them just because your dad does!" My heart beats hard.

Alkomso squints her eyes at me. "Fern—"

"What?" I say, a little too loud. "What?" I say again, softer.

Then she glances over my shoulder. "Hey," she says. "Where did the boys go?" She looks all around.

They're not at the bottom of the berm. They're not on the road. They're not with us.

A few yards down, the orange snow fence has been lifted up from the ground, creating a small gap.

"Oh no…" I race over to it. Sled marks. I get down on my belly to snake under fence and inside the work site.

Sure enough, Mikko, Abdisalom, and Alexi are fooling around with the sleds at the bottom of the pit.

"Get out of there!" I shout. Alexi waves up at me. "Come here! Right now!" I point to the ground at my feet. *"Now!"*

"Come and get us," says Alexi. "Nah, nah." He sticks his tongue out at me and then turns around and wiggles his butt. My whole mass of hair might turn gray in an instant.

"I am *not* kidding," I shout. "Get up here before you get hurt."

Just then, a bulldozer stops. The blade lowers to the ground. The man operating it steps outside his cab, takes off his hard hat, and stares at the boys. He yells something at them, but I can't hear what. He pulls a cell phone out of his pocket and taps it, then puts it to his ear.

"You guys are going to get us in big trouble!" I holler. "Come up here."

A siren wails. Red lights blink.

The boys startle and scramble for the berm, climbing like spiders up a wall.

Some workmen begin shouting at us. I can't quite make out what they are saying, but I'm sure it's not good.

The boys hike up, mud clumps thick as cement blocks clinging to their boots. When they're nearly at the top, I kneel down and reach out my hand.

The sirens keep screeching.

Alexi grabs my hand, and I pull him up and push him toward the gap in the fence. I do the same with Abdisalom and Mikko. Once his feet are through, I take one last look at the work site and at the men storming toward us.

"Sorry!" I shout. Then I get low and slither down the other side. "Let's *go*!" I grab Alexi's arm and Mikko's hand. Alkomso seizes Abdisalom's. We run.

After a while, Alkomso slows and bends over with her hands on her knees. "I can't run anymore. I have a side ache." She breathes heavily, stands up straight, and holds her stomach. "They're not following us anyway."

I listen hard, but I don't hear shouting or truck engines.

"That was so cool!" says Alexi.

Alkomso puts her face right up close to his. "You guys could have gotten hurt!"

"Those old men couldn't catch me," says Abdisalom. "I'm too fast."

"That was so stupid of you!" The words are out of my mouth before I can stop them. "What if Grandpa finds out what you did? Do you want to get taken away from your dad? Do you want to end up like Mark-Richard and Gary?"

My brothers look at me quizzically. I've never really explained to them about the struggles we're having at home. And I know Toivo has worked hard to keep them protected, too.

"You're hurting my ears," says Abdisalom. "Quit yelling."

"Be quiet, Abdi!" I say.

Alkomso takes his hand and glares at me. "Don't talk to him that way."

I swallow, not knowing what to say.

"I need to get home. I need to work on my project." She tugs Abdisalom along down the road. Before too long, they are swinging hands and Abdisalom is skipping next to her as though all is forgiven.

I nearly call out her name two or three times, but I don't. I'm mad at the boys. I'm mad at Grandpa. I'm mad at Toivo. And now Alkomso's mad at me, and I'm mad at her, too.

And, if Grandpa finds out about this, which he probably will, he's going to get even madder at Toivo, who's going to get mad at me for letting the boys out of my sight and making him look bad, and if we're all mad at one another, then what? What's the use in trying to keep my family together?

My brothers punch and poke at each other. They kick dirt at each other and throw rocks in each other's hair, as if they don't have a care in the world, as if they didn't just almost get us into big, fat trouble. I just about got all of us into big trouble, too.

I quicken my pace. My hands are freezing. I blow on them and then cross my arms over my chest and start walking. Marching, more like. I stare at the ground and don't look back to see whether the boys are following me.

I wonder what would happen if I just kept walking. Not go home. Not make them dinner. Not get them to bed. Not check their backpacks. Not walk them to school. What if I hid out in the woods? What if I built myself a small lean-to? What if I lived like Brian in *Hatchet*? I could do it. I could do it better than Brian, probably.

Or maybe I'll just walk all the way to end of the earth.

Chapter 13

I go on walking in a slumpy funk until I reach Horace Millner's property.

All the dogs stand in a line at the fence, almost as if they were waiting for me to show up. They are arranged from smallest to biggest. As I walk past each of them, they wag their tails or cock their heads. At the end of the row is Ranger. The dog with the big belly reaches her tongue forward to catch a water drop off the fence. Ranger barks, and she returns to her position.

Oh, great, I think. When he wants them to tame down, even Ranger is better at keeping control of his family pack than I am.

"What's the trick, huh, Ranger?" I stand on one side of the fence, and he sits on the other. We give each other a good once-over.

I crouch down so that we're eye to eye. Ranger makes a gravelly sound, but it doesn't seem angry. I reach out my hand. "Remember me?" I let Ranger sniff my hand. "I know you do. I'm the one who cut that duck off your neck."

Ranger moves his nose against my fingers. His nose is wet and cool, like a pebble pulled out of a creek. I pet his snout and rub his nose all the way up between his eyes. He presses his forehead into my hand, so I scratch his ears.

"That feels good, doesn't it," I tell him. I remember how Mom would rub my head and scratch my scalp a bit with her nails and comb through my hair with her fingertips when she put me to bed. I always loved that. I remember begging her to keep doing it until I fell asleep, and sometimes she would.

Ranger shivers, which makes me giggle. Shivering must be the dog way of getting goose bumps. Ranger is grateful for the smallest kindness. I scratch him harder and rub his ears, where his fur feels velvety, and then stroke him from ear to back and back to ear.

The high-pitched grinding of a truck shifting gears alerts all the dogs. At once, the entire pack lift their heads toward the road. Ranger's neck vibrates as he emits a low growl and then a high bark. *Danger* is what that means.

The boys.

A panicky chill tingles my spine.

"Mikko?" My air is short. I walk fast toward where they should be. "Alexi?"

When I see them horsing around in the middle of the road, I trot. I hear footsteps alongside me on the inside of the fence. Ranger darts in stride with me.

Then I see the truck coming up behind the boys.

"Alexi!" I run and wave my arms high above my head. They don't hear me, and they don't see me.

The engine revs higher.

My heart beats fast and loud and hard. I cup my hands around my mouth and yell, *"Get off the road!"*

But Mikko is down on all fours while Alexi sits on his back, pretending to whip him with a quirt and kick him like a bronco.

The big square shape of the truck barrels toward them.

I run faster. Ranger breaks away into a full-on run. He barks, not at me but at the boys.

The driver of the truck doesn't slow down. Either the driver can't see the boys, little and dirty and low in the middle of the road, or he's not paying attention.

Ranger picks up speed, more speed than I can keep up with.

The truck is so close to my brothers that I can make out the grille and the headlights. When my brothers look up and see me waving my arms, my throat seizes up so I can't get out another word.

Mikko and Alexi look behind them and spot the truck, but they don't move. They are frozen solid.

Then, far out ahead of me and past the boys, Ranger leaps over the fence. He runs across the ditch and up onto the road. He runs right at the truck.

My head pounds. My heart pounds. I stop.

The truck hisses as it slows down suddenly. The horn blows sharply.

But the squishing brakes and grinding metal and crunching gravel and blaring horn do not cover the sound of the tire hitting Ranger's body.

They do not drown out the sound of one yelp coming from Ranger's throat.

They do not hide the blast of air leaving Ranger's body as he hits the ground in a heap.

Mikko grabs Alexi and dives into the ditch. Snow and gravel fly up from the truck's tires as it swerves, dips down into the opposite ditch, and smashes into a tree. Glass breaks. Branches rattle and fall. Water sizzles on a hot engine.

I beeline for my brothers. In the ditch, they sit side by side with their arms around each other. Their faces are scratched from the rocks and snow. Alexi's eyes are glassy with tears that haven't fallen. His face is milky-colored and dull. I take him and pull him to my chest.

"It's okay," I say. "You're okay." My voice shakes, and my hands feel separate from me. I can see them clutching Alexi and Mikko, but I can't feel them at all.

"I'm sorry," Mikko says. "I'm sorry. I'm sorry." He gulps and then sobs loud and hard. His entire body shakes. Alexi is too stunned to cry, but the tears run down his face and onto my arm.

I rock them a little. "It's okay. Everything is going to be okay."

Toward the fence, footsteps crunch the snow and leaves. One by one, all the dogs in Ranger's pack walk up, and one by one, they sit down in the same order as before. They stare at the road. I press Mikko's and Alexi's heads to my chest and turn my own head toward the road.

Ranger lies on his side. A crimson stain spreads out beneath his body.

I bite down on my tongue and close my eyes. Mikko tries to turn to look. I put his head against my chest and don't let him.

Chapter 14

The driver of the truck rattles his door handle and pushes on the door. It's warped and won't open. He kicks it, and he hits the window. I have a sense that I should get up and help him, but my whole body is shaky and unsteady. If I tried to stand, I think I would fall down. I don't feel as though I can do anything but sit here in the ditch and hold on to my brothers. Mikko's sobbing has calmed into soft hiccups. Alexi puts his thumb in his mouth and sucks on it.

A few of Ranger's pack whine. The dog with the heavy belly howls sadly.

The driver opens his window and crawls through it.

He sits down on the road and calls over to us, "Are you kids okay?"

I nod yes.

He pulls a cell phone from his pocket and dials.

In a few minutes, sirens cut the air. Soon flashing lights twirl. At that, Mikko and Alexi perk up and slide out of my tight grip. Mikko has a fat lip, and red eyes from crying. Pink returns to Alexi's face.

I keep their backs to where I think Ranger landed. I don't want them to see. *I* don't want to see.

"My shoulder hurts," Alexi says. He uses his other hand to hold the shoulder and grimaces. I notice then that his right arm seems to be hanging off-kilter.

"Can you move it?" I ask.

"*Oh!*" he cries. He breathes hard and fast. "No. It hurts."

"Okay," I say. "Don't worry. We're going to get you fixed up."

A squad car screeches to a halt near the truck. An officer pops out of the vehicle and approaches the driver. "Are you all right?"

The driver points to us. "Take care of them kids," he says.

The officer nods and then walks toward us. He

slows down where Ranger lies in the road, shakes his head, and continues on. He kneels down beside us.

"How are we doing here?" he asks. He's young, and he seems a little nervous. "You hurt your arm?" he asks Alexi, who is holding on to his shoulder.

"Yeah," says Alexi. "That truck almost ran me over!" He rubs his shoulder. "And Mikko pushed me into the ditch. Hard."

The officer smiles with one half of his face. "Sounds like a rough day, pal." He looks at me. "These your brothers?"

"Yeah."

"Are you hurt?" he asks.

I gulp. The truth is that everything hurts right now. "Not really," I say. "Can you check on the dog? I mean, I know you're here for us, but can you? Will you, please?"

"Uh…" He shakes his head. "I'm sorry. I would if I could, but I can't."

I nod.

He sighs. "I'm really sorry. Well, the ambulance is on its way, and we'll get you all checked out. Sit tight." He heads over to his squad car.

As he puts orange cones around the whole scene,

another police officer and the ambulance arrive. The EMTs separate Mikko, Alexi, and me and give us each a thorough examination. Alexi gets strapped onto a stretcher and lifted into the back of the ambulance. Mikko sits in the back of the same ambulance, getting his lip cleaned up. An EMT shines a light in my eyes.

"You feel woozy?" she asks me.

"No," I lie. "I feel fine." My mouth fills with a metallic taste, and my stomach turns.

She smiles and pats my knee. "It's a good thing no one was seriously hurt," she says. "Coulda been a lot worse." She grabs my forearm and puts two fingers on my wrist. She stares at her watch.

"Did you happen to see if the dog was—"

She's looking at her watch, shushes me.

"Okay, that's fine!" She looks out at the scene on the road. "I've seen a lot worse. On this road, even."

Maybe she's talking about Mom, and maybe she isn't.

"Yeah" is all I can think to say. When she seems satisfied with my heart rate, she lets go. I sneak in between the EMTs and peer over their shoulders at my brothers, who are having lights shined in their eyes and ears. "Boys," I say, "don't be scared. I'm right here."

"I'm not scared," says Mikko, even though his eyes look scared.

"What happened to Ranger?" asks Alexi. "Is he okay?"

An EMT moves me out of the way before I can answer.

With my brothers in good hands, I go find Ranger. The closer I get, the stronger the aroma of blood. I'm used to it, of course, from butchering. Blood has a very curious, inside-out aroma. The only other smell that comes close is what you get when you dig a deep hole, like a grave.

The toe of my boot skims the outer edge of a pool spreading from under Ranger's head. The blood is already turning from crimson to a deep maroon. The side of Ranger that is faceup is perfectly whole. He could be just any old dog lying down for a lazy rest.

I circle the stain and kneel down at Ranger's head. His eyes and mouth are closed. I pet him. He's warm. His chest barely rises and falls.

He's alive. He's *alive*.

I pet him again between the eyes. Then I scratch his head and rub his velvet ears.

He opens his eyes and exhales loudly. "Thank you,

Ranger," I whisper, "for saving my brothers' lives." I rest my head on Ranger's head, let my gray hair fall over his gray hair. *Nerves of steel*, I think.

"Ah-*hem*," I hear. I look up.

Horace Millner.

With all the cars and commotion, I didn't notice him pulling up.

I sit back out of the way as Millner kneels down and puts his hand on Ranger's chest. He leans over and listens to his breathing and his heart. Millner inspects Ranger's leg, which is cockeyed and crushed. Then he wraps Ranger's body in an old wool army blanket, gently tucks his hands under the dog's body, and lifts him up like a baby. Ranger groans in pain.

"I'm so sorry," I tell Horace Millner. My voice shakes and my lip quivers, but I have to tell him. I have to say the words. "It's all my fault."

Horace's lips get tight and thin. His chin quivers.

"It's not your fault," he says.

I put my hand over my mouth and close my eyes.

"It was an accident," he says.

I open my eyes and peer at him. Somehow he seems much smaller and thinner than I thought. He adjusts the blanket over Ranger. "Fern?"

"Yeah?"

"I'm really sorry, too."

I look down at the ground and then at Horace Millner's boots. A drop of blood hits them.

"I know you are," I say.

Horace Millner sighs. "Come on, old boy," he says. "Let's take you home and see if we can't patch you up."

As Horace Millner walks away carrying that heavy load, he seems to take with him a heavy load of mine.

Chapter 15

Alexi gets to ride to the hospital in the ambulance. The police call Toivo. When they can't reach him on his phone, they ask if I know where else he might be.

"I'm not sure. Work, maybe?" I say. "Try Kloche's."

"Do you have anybody else we can call?" the officer asks. "A mom or an aunt? We'll put in a call, too, to social services, so there's someone to be with you until we find your family."

I pull Mikko close. "Grandpa, I guess."

Before you know it, what's an already-crowded country road has Toivo's white pickup, Gramps's big diesel, and Miss Tassel's Caprice parked nose to nose, as if they're about to race.

All three car doors slam at the same time. All three come running toward Mikko and me.

"Where's Alexi?" Toivo shouts.

"Is Alexi all right?" Grandpa demands.

"Are you all right?" Miss Tassel wants to know.

Mikko, scared and tired, shrinks into me and sighs. Toivo jogs ahead of Grandpa and Miss Tassel. When he gets to us, Toivo cups each of our faces and looks into our eyes.

"Thank God," he says.

A police officer lets Toivo and Grandpa and Miss Tassel know that Alexi has been taken to the hospital. Then Grandpa and Toivo get into an argument about whose fault it is. Toivo says a swear word. He says, "If you'd keep those *blankety-boom-boom* pipe trucks off the road, this wouldn't have happened!"

Grandpa says a swear word, too. "If you weren't such a *something, something* loser, my grandkids would be safe and sound with me!"

This goes on for some time until an officer walks over and stands between them, saying that he's going to arrest both of them if they don't knock it off and that there are more important things to worry about right now.

A wooziness comes over me, and I lean into Mikko and close my eyes. Miss Tassel kneels down beside us and tells us everything is going to be fine.

"Yeah, right," I say.

"Are we going to go to a foster home, too?" Mikko asks. "Like Gary?"

Miss Tassel doesn't respond right away. Instead, she rubs my back, which feels awkward. When I stiffen, she stops. "Sorry." She says she's going to talk to Gramps, Toivo, and the police and get us home for today.

"I want Alexi," says Mikko.

"Me, too," I say. Up from my stomach comes a retchy slime of bile. I swallow it down. But up it comes again. This time I turn my head and puke all over the ground. Mikko jumps away.

"Gross!" he shouts. But then he comes over and holds back my hair while I puke some more.

My throat and nose burn. Behind my eyes is a ballooning pressure. I heave again.

Everyone runs over to me. An EMT asks me if I hit my head earlier. I tell her no. Toivo says, "Poor girl." Grandpa says, "Let's get her off the road." Miss Tassel says she'll take us home while Grandpa and Toivo go to the hospital to be with Alexi.

Toivo and Grandpa can't find any way to argue with that, so that's what happens.

Toivo helps me to Miss Tassel's car. Grandpa carries Mikko over to it and buckles him up.

"I'll be home soon," says Toivo.

Beyond exhausted, I say, "I don't care. I want my brother back with me."

Toivo looks hurt. He closes the car door gently and speeds off to the hospital.

Late that night, long after Mikko and I are in bed, I hear Toivo return. Watching from my upstairs window, I see him carry Alexi, whose arm is in a sling, into the house. After a muffled conversation with Miss Tassel downstairs, she leaves quietly. I go back to bed.

Aside from giving him the details of what happened on the road, I give Toivo the silent treatment over the next couple of days. On top of all the unpaid bills and threats from creditors and Children's Protective Services material lie his hiring papers. The top one reads, WELCOME TO KLOCHE INDUSTRIES, THE WORLD LEADER IN NATURAL GAS EXTRACTION!

Toivo thinks I don't understand the constant itch of being poor, how it's always a bug biting your back in a place you can't reach. I do, though. Every morning, I'm the one darting my eyes over the cupboard, refrigerator, or freezer, gnawing my know-how for what to feed all of us. I don't complain about that. So why does being poor bother him so much? So much that he'd go and work with the polluters?

I sit on the couch, pretend to be watching TV, and brush my hair over and over again.

"Fern," he says, "I have to talk to you about something."

I ignore him.

"Did you hear me?" he says.

I grab my hair into a ponytail down my shoulder and furiously brush the ends. "You're the deaf one," I mumble.

He blinks and adjusts his hearing aid. "What did you say?"

"I said, *you're* the deaf one!"

He cocks his head and puts his hand on his hip. "What is that supposed to mean?"

I throw the brush onto the floor. "I saw you! I saw you at the fracking site!" I pause. And then I decide to let him have it. "At least Grandpa's honest. You're not! Maybe we *would* be better off with him."

Toivo walks over to the television and punches the Off button. "You're getting too big for your britches, missy."

"Whatever," I say.

His nostrils flare. "Fern."

I don't answer. I lie down on the couch and put a pillow over my face. The clean scent of freshly laundered and line-dried goodness fills my nose. Toivo must have done the laundry. *So what*, I tell myself. I bite the pillow to keep from screaming.

"Fern," he says again.

"Go away," I muffle.

Somehow Toivo hears that loud and clear. He leaves the room and goes into the kitchen. The refrigerator door opens and closes, and then a can top cracks open. Then nothing. I turn and peek out from beneath the pillow. He stands there with a beer can in his hand, staring out the window.

Go ahead. Drink it, I think.

He stands there for another minute. "That job pays fifty grand a year." He throws the full beer can into the sink, where it lands with a tin *thunk*. Beer and foam spill down the drain. He pulls a cigarette from the pack in his shirt pocket and goes outside, slamming the door behind him.

I sit up and tap my feet on the floor. A faint scent of cigarette smoke wafts from the doors and windows, which all need to be resealed. Or, better yet, replaced. For the first time, I wonder how much that costs.

As I pass the door on my way to my room, I stop and think about going out and talking to Toivo.

But I don't. I go upstairs, take the hottest shower I can stand, and then go to my room, where I slam my door, too.

I can't sleep. And it's not because of the trucks—they're not running. I lie there and make a list of all the things I have to worry about. From least important to most important. Then I think about them and shuffle them again.

The STEM fair is one thing on my mind. But it's the least of my worries.

So is Mr. Flores, who is trying to do something about the fracking problem.

And Toivo, who's making the fracking problem worse.

So is Alkomso, because she's making me wonder whose side to be on.

Alexi's wonky arm is on my mind, too, which is all my fault.

So is Mark-Richard, who didn't do anything wrong at all but was punished.

So is Horace Millner, who I've been so unfair to, whose dog might die, which is also all my fault.

So is Ranger. Who I might never see again.

And the woods, which is right in the middle of it all. Which might be cut down.

And Grandpa, who, if he has his way, will make sure I never see Toivo or the woods or Ranger again anyway.

I lie facedown. My pillow is damp from my freshly washed hair. Yuck. I flip it over and put my face back down. But when I close my eyes, there's Ranger on the road. The pool of crimson. The blood splatter, like a perfectly round rose hip, on Millner's boot.

I go to the window and lift it open. Cold wind blasts in and whips up my hair. For a while, I stay there with my eyes closed, leaning on the windowsill, as the breeze dries my hair. The stars sparkle above. Long, dark, wispy clouds blow across a half-moon, silver and gray.

Maybe there's this other place I don't know about, kind of like a heaven, I guess, or a garden or a forest where all the dead people and animals are having a nice time. Maybe it's up there in the sky. It's a pretty simple thought or hope, but on this night that goes by so slowly, the simple thought brings me a little peace.

I run my fingers through my hair, which is dry and cold, like metal. When my eyes finally get heavy, I lie back down in my bed and bury myself deep under the comforter.

Chapter 16

When I get to school the next morning, I drop the boys off at their classrooms, give Alexi's toad teacher the evil eye as I tell her why his arm is in a sling, and then bound up the stairs to my classroom.

Margot and her mom are whispering near her locker. Margot is holding on tight to her backpack and crying. Her mom is all dressed up in heels and a blazer, which is what she wears when she's subbing. I guess Mr. Flores isn't here. Maybe he's never coming back. Maybe Margot's mom finally got her way and got him fired. Nothing is going right.

I try to mind my own business, but then I hear Margot say, "It is *not* going to be all right!"

Those were almost the exact words I was just thinking. Then she adds, "I don't understand, and I never will!" And "Can't you and Dad just try one more time?"

I guess Margot Peterson's family is falling apart, too.

Mrs. Peterson cups Margot's chin. "You've got to get a hold of yourself now. The bell's going to ring. I have to get in there." Mrs. Peterson straightens her pencil skirt and clomps her three-inch heels into the classroom.

When I walk past Margot, I should keep going with my head down, the way I normally do, but she's heaving with crying. I gulp and stop.

She faces her locker, with her back to me.

"Margot?" I say softly. "Are you all right?"

She exhales loudly. "What do you care?" She glances over her shoulder to see who she's talking to. "Oh," she says. "It's you. Where's your best friend?"

My stomach flops at that. I'm not sure I even have a best friend anymore.

Margot wipes her nose and then her eyes on her sleeve. I'm about to walk away when she turns around, straightens her back, and lifts her chin. "I'm fine."

"Okay," I say. "Um...do you want me to go and get one of your friends?"

"Ha! They don't care. Marley said, 'Everyone's parents are divorced, so what the big deee-aaal, Margot?'"

"Oh." I need to get into the classroom, but I don't know what to do with Margot. "Um...I'm really sorry about your parents."

At that, her eyes fill with tears again. She fights back a sob. "Thanks," she barely gets out. She grabs my arm and I stand there, paralyzed. She digs her fingernails into my biceps. "I just don't understand," she says. "Parents are so selfish. Me and Kayla are going to have to live in different houses. Mom's moving to the city with Kayla. And I have to stay with Dad. For school. Kayla is only, like, three years old!"

"That's ridiculous," I say. It seems like all the kids I know are at the mercy of the whims of grown-ups.

She looks me right in the eye. Tears overflow hers. "Right? I mean, why do they have to separate us?" She wipes her tears away again. Sniffs. Then exhales. "Well, let's go before Mom gets mad and divorces me, too." She leans on me, and we walk into the classroom together.

The bell rings.

Margot scurries for her desk, and I dash for mine.

That's when I see that Alkomso has moved her desk right next to Mark-Richard's.

"Mark-Richard!" I say.

His cheeks redden. I smile at him and raise my hand and wave to him. He lifts his fingers in a small wave back. I know why he's feeling embarrassed. When you have to come back and face your whole class after the whole town's been talking, it's like you're a stuffed bird that everyone is studying. And while they're studying you, what everyone is thinking is, *Yuck.*

Between their desks, *Hatchet* lies open. But Alkomso's eyes are on me. She doesn't smile at me like she usually does. She looks from me to Margot and back again. I know what she's thinking, too. She's thinking that now I'm going to try and be friends with Margot again. Maybe she even thinks I'll start teasing her again. I want to explain, but there's no time. Mrs. Peterson says, "Good morning, class."

"Good morning," we say in staggered greetings. Everyone is looking around at everyone else. It's pretty hard to concentrate.

Margot Peterson has obviously been crying.

Mark-Richard is back after the fire.

I'm back after the crash.

"Where's Mr. Flores?" a kid asks.

Mrs. Peterson snaps her eyes up at us. "He's been put on leave."

"Why?" the kid asks.

"That's none of your business," says Mrs. Peterson.

Margot sneers. "Why don't you just tell everyone, Mom? Tell everyone how you get rid of people who don't agree with you."

Kids whisper and murmur. A lot of us put our heads down.

"Margot!" says Mrs. Peterson. "Don't start!"

She passes out a half sheet of paper with the STEM fair rubric on it, 100 points total. "Class," she announces, "this project-based assessment bears considerable significance." She stands at the front of the room, behind the podium. "And due to recent events, I must now implore you to look upon this assignment as your chief priority, as its outcome will be the sole factor in your final evaluation."

Kids knit up their eyebrows. Mark-Richard whispers "What?" to Alkomso.

Margot leans back in her seat, crosses her arms, and stares at her mother. "She just means that it's the only grade we get for science because Mr. Flores has been put on leave."

"Ooohhhh," goes the class.

"That's not fair," some kids whine.

"I haven't even started," someone says.

"Mine's terrible," another kid confesses.

And one student tells everyone, "Mine's done! My mom did the whole thing."

Mrs. Peterson glares daggers at her daughter. "Yes," she says. "What Margot expressed so simply is correct. But you can blame that on Mr. Flores, who for some reason never administered even one test for proper assessment."

"He said he didn't believe in tests," says Mark-Richard.

Mrs. Peterson rolls her eyes.

Kids keep talking and interrupting until Mrs. Peterson claps her hands together and tells everyone to quiet down. "As a concession, I have decided to give you the entire period to work on your projects," she says. "So get busy."

As everyone takes out their notebooks, I'm frozen in place. Doing a STEM project was scary enough, but now it's my entire grade. I might not even pass science if I don't do well, and that would for sure help Grandpa get me and the boys taken away from Toivo.

I peek over my shoulder now and again. Alkomso is talking with Mark-Richard, and I can tell by the way he's looking over her project that they're going to be partners.

When I open my backpack and pull out my note-book, I realize I brought the wrong one. This is Mom's recipe book.

I tap the eraser of my pencil onto the desk.

"Hey, Fern." Margot comes up and sits her butt on the corner of my desk.

"Yeah?"

"Your hair looks nice today." She holds up the ends of her hair and picks at them like she's pulling seeds off a puffy dandelion. "I wish I didn't have these frizzy split ends."

I smooth the top of my head. I'm not sure what to say. Normal people would respond with a thank-you, but I've still got my guard up. Sometimes when Margot gives a compliment, she's really just testing whether or not you agree with her compliment. Then she goes behind your back and says that you "think you're all that."

"I like your hair," I tell her. I clear my throat. "I wish mine were blond like yours. With the pink color, too."

Her face lights up. "No way! Mine is a rat's nest." I know that she doesn't really think that. I know that we're really just playing a dumb communication game. "Um," she goes on, "um, have you started your project?"

"Well…" I point at my notes with the tip of my pencil. "No."

She leans over and reads my mom's writing. I move my hand so she can't see.

"What is it? Like a recipe book or something?" She adjusts a hair clip behind her ear.

"Yeah," I say. "I guess so. It was my mom's."

"What's a groundnut?" she asks.

"Food you can find in the forest."

"Oh," she says. "That sounds like a cool project."

"It's not my pro—" I begin. And then I think about it. "Thanks, Margot. I hope so. I hope it is a cool project."

"I'd be your partner, but I don't like to go outside and get dirty collecting food and whatever." She scans the room and waves at a girl named Emily, who has a birthmark on her cheek that Margot calls a "skunk punch." Emily raises three fingers and waggles them in an uneasy wave back. Then Margot zips toward her.

I guess Margot is feeling like her old self a little bit. "Psst!"

I look over my shoulder. Alkomso smiles at me and lifts up her hands like *What's her deal?*

I just shrug. Alkomso rolls her eyes in a way I can tell is about Margot and not me, and then she turns back to Mark-Richard and her project. Maybe she's not quite so mad at me anymore.

Chapter 17

At the end of the day, Alkomso, Mark-Richard, and I meet like we used to before picking up our little brothers. We stand in a circle. Neither Alkomso nor I say anything. She adjusts and readjusts her hijab, and I pretend to be fiddling with the zipper on my backpack.

Mark-Richard's new shoes don't smell like raisins. He's got a new coat on, but he's got a long-dog face. He looks from Alkomso to me, maybe wondering why we're acting so strangely.

"Boy," he says, "it sure is great to see you guys again."

"You, too!" says Alkomso.

"Yeah," I add. "We were really worried about you and Gary."

Mark-Richard's eyes get watery.

"You all right?" I ask. "I saw your house."

He shrugs his shoulders. "I've been better."

"Where are you living?" asks Alkomso.

"With this family on the other side of Colter. They're nice. I have my own room."

I don't know if I should ask about his parents or not, so I don't.

"What about Gary?" asks Alkomso.

"He's with a different foster family. The ones who took my little sister, Hattie. It's nice they get to be together." He smiles tightly. "But that family was too full to take me, too."

My tongue feels swollen. Like I can't talk, and I worry that anything I say will just sound dumb. So I just nod.

Alkomso says, "Do you want to come with me to pick up Abdi?"

"And Mikko and Alexi are dying to see you," I add.

After we get the boys, we all head outside. But instead of walking home with us, Mark-Richard moves toward the bus lines. "I gotta go so I don't miss the bus." Mikko wraps his arms around Mark-Richard's waist and squeezes him. Mark-Richard hugs him back. "Bye, buddy. See you tomorrow."

Off he goes to get on the bus, which will take him the opposite way from where he used to live. He looks smaller, somehow, without Gary trailing along with him.

Alkomso and I herd our little brothers away from school. For a while we don't talk about anything. So much has happened since our argument that our argument doesn't seem all that important anymore.

Finally she says, "So, I guess you and Margot Peterson are BFFs again." She gives me a kidding punch on the arm.

I laugh. "Not quite," I say. "Her parents are getting divorced."

"That sucks," says Alkomso. "But I'm not ready to be quite as nice as you are." She shifts her backpack on her shoulder and clears her throat. "You pick a STEM project yet?"

"Maybe." After a few more steps, I add, "How's yours coming?"

"Good." She doesn't go on about it. "I'm glad you didn't get hurt in the accident," she says. "That must have been really scary."

"It was. The dog got hurt bad." I lower my voice so the boys can't hear. "I don't think he'll make it."

"I hate when dogs die! Even if it's just in a book. It's the worst."

At her apartment we say good-bye, pretty much like old times, but not exactly. Something has definitely changed between us. It was easier when we agreed about everything.

But now I have to have my own mind. And she has to have her own mind. And somehow we have to figure out how to be a different kind of friend to each other.

As we approach Millner's woods on our way home, I'm secretly hoping that I'll see Ranger running and jumping and being his dog self. But I know that probably isn't going to happen.

My brothers and I stop when we see a Subaru wagon parked on the side of the road and a sign tacked onto Millner's fence. YOU CAN'T FRACK MY LAND is what it says.

"I know what that says," says Mikko. "It says, 'You can't f-f-f—'"

"Frack," I say.

Mikko gives me a side eye. "Oh," he says. "'You can't frack my land.'"

"Very good, kiddo."

Off in the distance, there's a commotion of barking and yipping. Ranger's pack. My heart jumps. Alexi puts his fingers in the corner of his mouth and whistles. "Here, doggies!" he shouts. "Here, pups!"

While we wait, the crashing of legs breaking branches scatters the birds out of the trees.

"They're coming," says Mikko. He climbs up and over Millner's fence. "I'm going to catch one." Alexi crawls underneath the fence because his arm is wrapped up to his side.

I flip my legs over the fence rails.

A few of the fast dogs bust through the underbrush and circle Mikko and Alexi.

Whoo-hoo-hoo, they bark. *Ark! Ark! Ark!*

Ranger's not with them.

Not only is he missing, but the dog with the fat belly is gone, too. My heart falls, and I get a little stomach-sick thinking that he's suffering, trying to hold on to his life, or, worse, that he might be dead.

Mikko and Alexi kneel down and pat their legs. They know the dogs aren't mean-barking. They're just showing off and maybe saying hello or wanting to play. The tails of the dogs wag so fast that they shake the dogs' bodies. Without Ranger to boss them, the dog pack jumps and claws and wiggles. The dogs don't know which person to get attention from first, me or Mikko or Alexi. They sniff my hand and then Mikko's, and then go from smelling Alexi's butt to my boots.

"Hey!" a man shouts. "Boys! Come back here!"

Out from where the dogs came appear Millner and another man, all bundled up against the cold in a heavy coat with furry hood. A camera with a huge lens dangles from the man's neck.

"Uh," says Millner. He looks surprised. "Hey there, kids."

"Fern?" The other man puts his hood down.

"Mr. Flores?" It's weird when you see someone you know pretty well outside of the place that you know them from. "Hi. How are you? Are you coming back to school soon?"

"What are you doing out here?" he asks.

"Oh," I say, "I just, um, wanted to see about a dog."

Millner flits his eyes away from me. "He don't look too good, but he's hanging on."

"Oh," I say. "I wish—"

"Nothing you could have done about it," Millner interrupts. "Dog's had a good long life."

I swallow hard.

Mr. Flores lifts his camera and points it at the boys and the dogs. *Click. Click. Click.* "How's the project coming?" He stares at the back of his camera, clicks a bunch of buttons, leans over to show something to Millner.

Millner nods and laughs. "Good shot."

"I haven't really started," I tell Mr. Flores. "I have an idea, but not much else."

"Ought to get a shot of that owl burrow, too," says Millner to Mr. Flores.

Millner and Mr. Flores seem busy, as though they're doing something important. I'd like to know what, but I don't want to be nosy. "We'll get going now," I say. I try to get Mikko's and Alexi's attention, but they're busy getting jumped on by the dog pack. Alexi gets knocked over by a mutt with a crooked tail. The dog stands over Alexi and licks his face all over.

"Want to tag along?" Mr. Flores asks me. "We're taking pictures of all the important animal habitats out here."

"Show them to that dang city council," Millner

adds. "Thinking they can come in here and take my land for a bog of poison." He spits onto the snow. "No sirree."

"That's my project!" I say. "Kind of. I was going to do the foods of the forest for the STEM fair."

Mr. Flores smiles so big I can see the fillings in his back teeth. "Fern, that's great! That's what I'm talking about! A project that impacts your community! And now that I'm not officially your teacher, maybe I can lend a hand."

"Me, too, all right," says Millner. "Count me in. If you'll take my help, that is."

"I'd—" I stop. Take a deep breath and exhale. "I'd like that."

We walk around for a while, with Millner pointing out where the foxes den and where the raccoons wash their food and where the deer bed down. He even points out where the bear comes and scratches his back against a tree. Millner points out the currant, raspberry, and gooseberry bushes and the wild-plum tree.

I already know where they all are, but I say thanks anyway.

Chapter 18

For a few days our house is chilly, and not only because the windows and doors are drafty and the wind's now coming in from the frozen north. Toivo and I are polite to each other, but that's about it. When we pass each other in the tiny kitchen, we turn sideways and say, "'Scuse me." Instead of gushing over the venison roast and ramp supper, Toivo delicately wipes the corners of his mouth with a paper towel and says, "I really appreciate you fixing us the meal."

He leaves for work at the same time we leave for school, but even though he knows that I know where he's going, I don't say, "Have a great day at work!"

When he comes home from work and sees a bunch of photographs and descriptions of the edible plants in Millner's woods spread out on the table, he doesn't ask me how my project is going. Instead, he wanders around, sprays everything with Pledge and Lysol, and uses his shirtsleeve as a dust cloth. He swipes a broom along the corners of the ceiling, destroying cobwebs and ladybug shells. The whole while, he whistles old country songs. In the evenings, he sets the boys up on his lap and reads Dr. Seuss to them while they pick their noses and scabs.

Inside me there's a boiling stew of confused thoughts. Why's he cleaning so much? Why's he reading to the boys? Is this the way it's always going to be now?

By the weekend, I'm about burst. Just as I'm ready to try to talk to him, Miss Tassel's Caprice pulls into our yard.

I set my elbows on the ledge of the bedroom window and watch. Miss Tassel shuts off her car and scoops up some papers from the passenger seat and the floor. She holds them to her chest with one hand as she adjusts the rearview mirror with the other hand, then fluffs her hair up way high.

So this must be the home-inspection day. This is why Toivo's been cleaning up the house. I completely forgot that I was going to do it myself.

I tiptoe down the steps and settle with a creak on the last one. Toivo snaps his head to where I am crouched in the dark stairwell.

When she knocks on the door, Toivo goes and opens it. "Mornin'," he says.

"Good morning," she says. "All set?"

"I guess so." He suddenly looks very small to me. He's skinny as a string bean. I start to feel rotten that I was so snotty to him.

Miss Tassel drops a load of files and bags onto the kitchen table. "This all right here?"

Toivo nods.

She sniffs. "Smells clean in here."

Toivo tucks a wayward corner of his button-up—a new work shirt that has KLOCHE's embroidered on it—into his pants. "Uh, over here is the TV room. I mean, this is the room with the TV in it," says Toivo. He must be nervous as a cat at a coyote party. "I know it's a small house." He sighs. "But there's an upstairs, too."

"Mmm-hmm." Miss Tassel's stomach growls. Loudly. "Oh my!" she says. "Excuse me!" It growls again.

I slap my hand over my mouth to keep from laughing.

"Didn't have time to eat," she explains.

"I made some turkey jerky," Toivo says. "You want some of that?"

"Oh, I couldn't. I shouldn't."

"I insist," Toivo says.

"Well…." She hesitates. "All right. I am feeling a bit faint."

"Oh, and Fernny made currant jam. It's good if you dunk the jerky in it."

"That sounds delicious," says Miss Tassel. "Now, let's begin."

Toivo pulls out a chair for Miss Tassel and then gets the jerky and jam and a couple of paper towels. He sits down. First he puts his hands on the tabletop, then he puts them in his lap, and then he puts them back up on the table.

"Mr. Heikkenen, do you enjoy being a father?" asks Miss Tassel.

"What?" says Toivo. "I mean, of course I do, ma'am. I love them kids."

"Right," says Miss Tassel. "Most fathers do love

their kids. But some of them are not cut out for the day-to-day job of being a father."

Toivo doesn't respond.

"Mr. Heikkenen, what do you like most about being a father?"

"Ah—" he starts. "Um...ma'am?"

It's quiet again.

"Mr. Heikkenen," she says, "do you think you can provide for these children?"

"Well," he begins. He folds his hands together. "Well, I got a job."

I grind my teeth.

"But I'm not sure it's a good fit for our family."

I grab a clump of hair and suck on the ends of it.

"I see," says Miss Tassel. "Mr. Heikkenen, keeping a job is very important. Very important. Do you understand that?"

"Yes. I do."

"Okay. Let's move on. Do you think you can ensure that the children make it to school on time every day and that their homework is done toward grade-appropriate benchmarks?"

A few seconds pass in silence. I know Toivo is

working out the meaning of her words. "Ah, what, now, ma'am?" he says very softly.

"Mr. Heikkenen, your father-in-law says that you have a drinking problem, as well as post-traumatic stress disorder, and that you were wounded in Iraq and are no longer able to hold a steady job. Are these statements true?"

No word.

"Mr. Heikkenen, Fern—the girl—is not your natural daughter, is she?"

This time the silence goes on for about a minute. Miss Tassel opens the lid of my jam and then untwists the tie on the bag of jerky. She slides one out, dunks it, and takes an enormous bite. "Mmm. Mr. Heikkenen, tell me how you made this."

"Oh, um," says Toivo. "Well, ma'am. The boys and me have been tracking the wild turkeys for about a year now. So last month when our freezer meat was getting spare, we went out bow hunting."

"You let the boys use real bows and arrows?" Miss Tassel asks.

"What?" says Toivo.

I wonder if Miss Tassel knows about Toivo's hearing problem. He's too proud to tell her, I'm sure.

She repeats the question.

"No," he says. "I hit the birds. The boys help after."

"Oh. I see. Go on."

Toivo waits a bit. Then he continues. "So, I pegged two big toms in less than an hour. Each of the boys threw one over their shoulders. Boy, was that funny. Those toms weighed forty pounds each. But Mikko just had to carry one, and Alexi had to prove to his brother that he could, too. Then Fernny and I butchered them in the garage out back. And then, see, you have to filet some of the—"

"Okay," interrupts Miss Tassel. "That's enough, Mr. Heikkenen."

"Oh. Sorry, ma'am."

"No," says Miss Tassel, "I mean that really is good. It's good you're teaching your sons your traditions."

A chair shuffles around, and Toivo coughs into his fist. I can tell he's nervous.

"Ma'am?" he says.

"What is it?"

"Since I was twenty-six, I have been a father. First, when I fell in love with their mother, I became a father to Fernny. I had just got back from Iraq, and that woman and girl became my family." He stops. "My everything."

"Go on," says Miss Tassel.

191

"It was hard sometimes to get used to knowing how to be around a kid, but I came along all right, I guess, because I never had a day where I didn't love Fernny."

She nods. She takes another jerky. "But you never formally adopted her, right?"

"No. I guess I didn't. I guess I should have."

"You regret that?" she asks.

He stares out the window. "I do," he says. "There are other things I wish I had done better, too. I wish I hadn't drank so much in front of her. And same with the smoking. But mostly I have kept my language clean, so that's one thing I have in my favor. I also have in my favor that I have taught her to be self-sufficient about some things, which is not a thing they teach in school and lots of parents don't even know themselves anymore."

I hold my breath for a few seconds because I don't want to miss a single word.

"She can tell the difference between what you can eat and what will poison you out in the woods." He clears his throat again.

Miss Tassel taps a pen on the table.

I breathe.

"Anyway," Toivo goes on, "then I became father

to Mikko, Alexi, and Matti, all right in a row. It never occurred to me to separate between which ones were my kids and which one wasn't. I have always just thought that we belong together. I don't think of them as that one is her kid and these are my kids. I think of us as a family, and we all watch out for each other." He leans forward in his chair. "With or without adoption papers."

Miss Tassel rummages around in her purse. She pulls out a crumpled tissue, dabs her eyes, and blows her nose.

"Uh, then, as you know," he says, after a pause, "Johanna and Matti had an accident. Now they are gone to heaven, if there is one, and I hope that there is, because I would give anything to be able to see them at least one more time. But I don't know about the truth in that, which is a terrible thing to live with."

He coughs and sniffs. He's quiet, so quiet that the ticking of the clock and the humming of the refrigerator seem loud.

"Take your time," says Miss Tassel.

He clears his throat. "The world is hard," he starts again. "I do not want the kids to have hard lives. But I don't want them to have easy lives, either. The kids will struggle with me—that is true. But it is a good and honest kind of struggling that we do, one that makes us work together and pull out the best qualities in each of us. I can improve, and I will."

Miss Tassel nods. She leans forward, too. "Your father-in-law. He wants all of the children with him, you know."

Toivo sighs. "I am not stupid," he says. "I mean, I know that Big John will have an easier time taking away Fern than he will the boys. Because he's right— she doesn't share my blood." Toivo stops and looks to where I am in the dark. "But let me tell you and him something that no blood test will show. Behind her ear grows a patch of gray hair that comes from me." He points on his head to where my gray hair grows on mine. "He might say it comes from the stress I have caused that girl, and it is true she has had an unfair share of it. But I think—and I think she would agree with me on this—that that gray hair is mettle. She and I have had to scrounge and scrap to feed this family, and it takes courage to do that. I like to think that gray hair is a little bit of me in her. If Fern ever disagrees, I won't stop her from going. But I want her here, and here is where she belongs. I know Johanna would agree."

My heart and my lungs swell up like resting dough.

I spread my fingers and use them to comb through my gray hair.

It is nothing but quiet again. Finally, Miss Tassel opens up her file and begins writing. Toivo leans over to Miss Tassel's shoulder.

"I'll let you read it when I'm done," she tells him.

"Sorry," Toivo says.

"Don't worry," she says. "It's all good."

Chapter 19

A moment later I can hear a truck rumbling down the road. At first I think it's a fracking truck, but as the engine gets louder, I recognize the distinctive chugging of Grandpa's big diesel. I leap up and emerge from the stairwell.

"Well, hi there," says Miss Tassel. Everything on her face is wide in surprise.

"Grandpa's here," I tell Toivo. Like old habit, I feel I've got to get between the two of them.

"Sounds like it."

"Maybe you should go out back or something," I say to him.

Grandpa's knocking shakes the whole wall. I dash to the door and open it. Though Grandpa takes up nearly the whole doorframe, in the gaps I can see the rustling of dogs in the yard.

"What in the heck are all these dogs doing here?" Grandpa says. "Every one of them looks flea-bitten."

Like a swarm of bandits, Millner's dogs jostle around our house, biting at one another. Without Ranger, they don't know the dog rules anymore.

"They're okay, Grandpa."

Grandpa turns around and roars, "Get out of here! Yah! Yah!"

The dogs roar in return, shouting *woof, woof* with their long snouts poised like megaphones. Grandpa puts up his hands and yells, "Get! Get!" but the dogs don't listen. They circle his truck, peeing on all the tires.

Grandpa shakes his head in disgust and kicks some gravel and dust at them. They bark and howl.

I don't want him in the house, but I don't want him riling up the dog pack, either. "Grandpa, why don't you come in," I say.

Grandpa takes off his hat as he walks in and pats down his glossy hair.

"Big John," Toivo says. "What are you doing here?"

"Heard the inspection was today," says Grandpa. "Wanted to come over and make sure everything—and I mean *everything*—was taken into account." His boots clomp on the floor. He's stern-faced at Miss Tassel. "You the little lady who's conducting this inspection?"

One corner of her mouth turns down. "You can call me Dr. Tassel," she says. "I have two—that's right, *two*—doctoral degrees from the University of Michigan." Her chair scrapes the floor. She stands and extends her hand. "I am pleased to make your acquaintance, Mr....?"

Grandpa takes it and gives it a shake. "Firm grip you have there," he says, ignoring her question.

"My father was a general in the army, sir. He couldn't abide a weak handshake."

"I see," says Grandpa. He's coming down a little bit. Miss Tassel evens out some of Grandpa's gruff. "I'm Big John, the children's grandfather, owner of Greene Incorporated."

"Oh yes," says Miss Tassel. "I know of you. My secretary has passed along many of your messages."

"And I want to make sure that you take a look at every bankbook, every credit score, and every bill collector that this son of a gun has had any interaction with." Grandpa's voice rises like a raccoon up a tree. "He ruined my daughter's life, and I will not allow him to ruin my grandchildren's, too!"

"For God's sake, Big John—" Toivo says.

But Miss Tassel interrupts before Toivo can protest more. "I appreciate your concern, Mr. Greene, but as I said—or maybe I didn't say—I don't need your help. I know how to do my job."

"I want you to take photographs of the mold in the basement and take a square-footage measurement of this rinky-dink house that isn't big enough for one of my horses, much less my three grandkids. And that crap he feeds these kids. My God! I wouldn't feed it to my dogs."

"Grand—" I begin.

He turns to me. "Now, Fern, you stay out of this."

"But, Grand—" I try again.

"*Fern*," he scolds, "I told you to stay out of this. Go to your room."

Toivo steps forward. "Don't tell her what—"

Grandpa steps up to Toivo with a meaty pointer finger aimed at his face. "Don't *you* ever tell me what to do!"

"*Mr. Greene!*" Miss Tassel's got her hands raised, fingers splayed. "That is quite enough. Stand down, and I am not going to ask you twice!" Grandpa gasps, but Miss Tassel keeps going. "I am well qualified to handle this situation, thank you very much. And for your information, I myself grew up in a rinky-dink shack in Kentucky without electricity or indoor plumbing."

"Well, that's fine for you, but—" goes Grandpa.

Again, Miss Tassel pays him no mind. "We ate crawfish and shrimp and collard greens and beets," she says, "all pulled out of the water or the ground by me and my brothers." Grandpa stands there with his hands as big as dinner plates on his hips, his chest cocked slightly forward. It's his intimidation pose. Except Miss Tassel doesn't look intimidated. "And now I have two PhDs, so you'd best mind your tone with me, sir!"

I'm shocked, paralyzed, and completely impressed. I have never, ever heard anyone talk to Grandpa that way. Even Toivo stands with his mouth hanging open.

When I can finally breathe again, out comes a chuckle. "Wow," I say to no one in particular.

"Miss Tassel." Grandpa hangs on to the *s* in *Miss* and practically spits out the *T* in *Tassel*. "These children are not keeping up with their studies, and it is *his* fault. My daughter would not have wanted these grand-babies of mine failing school!"

"I understand your concern, Mr. Greene. I really do. But you've got to let me do my job here."

"Well, you'll be hearing from my lawyer if this doesn't turn out the right way," Grandpa says. The screen door slams.

I run to the window to watch. He stomps across the yard.

Miss Tassel isn't through with him yet, though. She goes to the kitchen door and shouts, "Go ahead! I'm working on a law degree, too!"

Grandpa slaps the hood of his truck and kicks a tire. He rumbles up his diesel engine and tears out of our gravel driveway, kicking up dust.

Chapter 20

As Grandpa tears off, Toivo fiddles with his hearing aid. "Don't worry, okay? Big John will calm down."

I nod. No matter how nasty Grandpa is to Toivo, Toivo never says a bad word about him—not to me at least. Maybe self-control is something they teach you in the military.

Miss Tassel wipes her hands off on her pant legs. "Your jam is out of this world! Did you find the berries yourself?"

"Yep," I say. "Yes, I mean. Out there." I point out the window toward the grove.

"That's wonderful. My brothers and I used to trap and scrounge, too. I miss it. Someone should write down all the things you can find out there."

"I am, actually. For the STEM fair. I'm going to make a field guide to all the edible food out there."

Toivo grins. Miss Tassel looks at Toivo, and she smiles, too. "What a wonderful idea."

A wave of relief washes over me, as though I just passed an enormous test.

Miss Tassel turns to Toivo. "Mr. Heikkenen, could you give Fern and me some privacy for a little while?"

Toivo raises his eyebrows. "What? I'm sorry. I didn't hear you."

Miss Tassel points to the door.

"Oh, you want me to leave you alone? Yes, ma'am. Gotcha." He grabs his pack of smokes and heads outside.

Miss Tassel watches the door close behind him. She turns to me and zeros in on my eyes. "It's all right if we talk for a minute, right?"

I swallow and blink. My teeth feel too tight for my mouth. "Yeah," I manage to say. I lay my hands in my lap and then plop them on the table and then fold them back on my legs.

"Must run in the family," she says. She leans forward across the table. "Fern, are you happy here?"

"Mostly." It's almost a whisper.

"Are you sad here?" she fires back.

I hesitate, and I wonder if this is a trap. I decide to tell the truth. "Yes," I drum my fingers on my thighs. "Sometimes. But isn't that normal?"

She ignores my question.

"Do you feel safe here?"

"Yes."

"Do you feel unsafe here?"

"Never. Unless there's a terrible storm or something that can't be controlled."

She flips open a file and slides out six or seven pieces of paper. "Now, where did I put my pen?" She searches her purse and scours her briefcase.

"It's behind your ear," I say. "Stuck in your hair."

She feels for it. "Oh yeah," she says. "Thanks." Miss Tassel licks the tip of the pen and scribbles checks in boxes on the paper. "Okay," she says. "One last question."

I sit very still and stare at the tip of her pen, in the air above the box she needs to check. She wiggles it a bit.

"Fern, when you think about the kind of adult you want to be someday, the goals that you have, do you think Toivo is the father who can help you achieve those goals?"

Blink. Blink. Blink.

Miss Tassel has long nails that are painted orange. On the very tip of each thumb is a gold stripe.

"Fern?" she says.

What kind of an adult do I want to be?

The kind who cares about her family.

The kind who can take care of her family.

The kind who works hard and has dirty fingernails and a stocked cupboard to show for it.

The kind who is smart and has a good job, maybe as a science teacher like Mr. Flores or a marine like Toivo.

"Fern?" Miss Tassel asks again.

"Yes," I say. "I can reach those goals with Toivo as my dad."

"Okay." She smiles. She checks the box. And then she reaches over and takes my hand. "You understand we have a problem, right? You know that the law is fussy about guardianship, right?"

"Yes."

"Is this where you want to be? With Toivo?"

It hits me like a winter gale. "Yes. I get mad at him sometimes, and I don't like that he's working for the frackers, but yes."

"And what about Grandpa?"

"I don't mind seeing him when he's not trying to take us away," I say. "I used to like seeing him sometimes." My entire body relaxes. It feels so good to just be able to say these things out loud to someone who really listens. My stomach even growls, and I remember I've not eaten anything all day. I remember I've hardly eaten anything for several days. I clutch my arms around my middle.

Miss Tassel smiles. "That's what I thought." She rubs her stomach. "I'm hungry, too. Sometimes I forget to eat when I'm stressed."

"Me, too!" I say. I go to the fridge and open it. The bare lightbulb shines down on a whole bunch of shelves that are bare except for a half-empty bottle of ketchup, a couple of shriveled apples, and some cheap slices of cheese. I spy a few jars way in the back. I grab one and put it on the table.

Miss Tassel straightens up and unscrews the lid from the pickled ramp bulbs. She smells inside the jar. She pulls out a ramp, a white bulb with a flat green stem. "Onion?" she asks.

"Pickled ramp," I correct her.

"Ramp? What in the world is a ramp?" She puts the ramp up to the light and turns it round and round.

"It's kind of like onion crossed with garlic."

She pops the whole thing in her mouth and chews. Vinegar drips down her lips. "Hmmm. Why have I never heard of these?"

"They grow in the woods in the spring. They look a little like lilies, but you can smell the difference pretty easy."

"You found this in the woods?"

"Yeah. Lots of them."

She licks her fingertips and then spins the jar, stirring up the mustard seeds and caraway. She scoops up another ramp and chomps it. Then she fishes out another. Miss Tassel points at her mouth. "These are good. Crispy."

"My mom taught me."

Miss Tassel sorts through her paper circus. "You know what would be delicious with these? Crawfish on crackers."

"Mikko and Alexi sometimes find crayfish in the pond in Millner's woods. Is that like a crawfish?"

"Yes!" she says, smiling. "Seriously? I haven't had a good crawdad in ages. You find them out there? In those woods?"

I nod. "Not for much longer, though, probably, if those frackers ruin it."

The smile drops from her lips. "Now that would be too bad. I wonder what folks would think about that if they knew about all the plants and animals out there. Anyway, what do you know about fracking?" she says.

"I know Kloche's is going to turn my grove into a wastewater pit." I put my chin up. "And I know that Mr. Flores thinks Kloche's is a bunch of polluters."

"Hmm," she says. "I've heard fracking causes earthquakes. They say it starts your drinking water on fire. Who knows?"

"That's terrible!"

She shrugs. "I see both sides of the fracking argument, though. Overall, from what I know, fracking is cleaner than coal, that's for sure." She picks at her teeth. "Got my daddy and just about every brother of mine suffering of lung disease from the coal mines of Kentucky." She swallows. "But you know what? That coal mine bought my education."

She takes her shoe off, scratches her foot. Then she slips her shoe back on.

I hesitate. But before I can stop them, the words are coming out of my mouth: "Toivo says he can make a lot of money."

"I see." She takes off her other shoe and wiggles her toes. She presses her toes against the floor until they all crack. Then she wiggles them again before she stuffs her foot back into the shoe. "I gather you're not too fond of the way he's making it."

"I don't want him to be stressed out about money," I say. "But I don't want Millner's woods to get cut down, either."

She stares at me as though waiting for me to continue. "I don't have to tell you this because you're smart enough to know it, but adults have to choose between a rock and another rock all the time."

"And a hard place?" I correct her.

"That, too," says Miss Tassel.

A small mouse dashes along the floorboard near the table. I hope she doesn't notice. I hold very still.

But Miss Tassel spies it out of the corner of her eye. "Looks like you need a cat," she says matter-of-factly.

My shoulders relax. "Mikko's allergic."

"A dog would do," she says.

"Yeah," I say. "It would."

"Fern," she says, "don't ever be ashamed of being poor. I've never met a strong woman who had an easy go of things early on."

I remember Toivo saying the same thing. "Thanks, Miss Tassel."

"But don't be too hard on Toivo for trying to get you out of it with an honest day's labor. And the labor of a man who is trying to feed and house his kids is honest."

I just listen.

"I'm gonna tell you something because you're smart and I think you can handle it," she says. "It's wonderful to have principles. But adults have to eat theirs all the time when life gets on them. You can't be so hard on people, Fern."

The scalp behind my ear burns. *Cut the duck off Toivo* is what she's telling me.

Chapter 21

Toivo buys me construction paper, new scissors, and a hot-glue gun for my project. Probably that wouldn't be a big deal to most people. But it wasn't too long ago that buying little things like those wasn't possible in our household.

I make pencil sketches and write descriptions of my edible plants, roots, and mushrooms, kind of like baseball cards, and hot-glue them on my display. I have some photos, too, from Mr. Flores, for where the plants can be found.

I've got one day to get this done. Tomorrow night the school will host the annual STEM fair. For today, I try not to think about the questions the judges will ask me. I try not to think about the other parents who will look at my project. I try not to think about all the other kids' projects or how much better they're going to be. I try not to think about how this project is my entire science grade for the whole year.

I do try to think that if I do a great job, maybe Grandpa will loosen that belt buckle a notch, relax, and give up his war against Toivo.

And I do try to think that maybe, just maybe, someone will like my project enough that they'll think it's important to save Millner's woods, too.

Alexi and Mikko tear around the house, chasing each other in a game they call Walnut Smear. They've stuffed their coat pockets with walnuts that fell to the ground and got snowed on, so the green covering is soggy and stinking up the house. Wherever a walnut lands, a green stain gets left. Mikko runs past me and trips on the hot-glue gun cord, sending the glue gun flying across the kitchen.

"Hey!" I scold. "Watch it!"

Alexi heaves a walnut at Mikko. He misses and hits the couch. *Splat.* From the inside of his sling, he pulls out another one, winds up, throws, and smacks Mikko right in the chest. *Splat.* Mikko scrambles after it, picks it up, and fires it back at Alexi. He misses and smacks the refrigerator.

"Knock it off!" I shout.

Alexi holds up another walnut.

"Don't even think about it," I warn him.

He leans against me and wipes his nose on my sleeve. He stares at the cards. "I want to help." He holds his walnut up to the card I made about walnuts. "You should glue this on there. I'll do it." He grabs for the glue gun.

"No way. That's hot! You could get burned."

"Can we go to Abdisalom's house, then?"

"No," I say. The boys are driving me crazy. "I really need to finish this. Can you guys just be good for a while? Why don't you watch TV?"

"This board looks too boring," says Alexi. "It needs better stuff on it."

I shake Alexi's head off my arm. I step back and stare at my board. Is it boring? I have my title, FOODS OF THE FOREST, in black construction-paper cutouts across the top middle. Then I have PLANTS on the left. ROOTS in the bottom center. MUSHROOMS on the top right. And NUTS on the bottom right.

Mikko comes over to criticize, too. "Yeah, you need to jazz it up."

"I do not," I say. "Go outside and quit being pests."

Alexi points to my sketch of a shaggy mane mushroom, which has a stalk and then a large cap. "Why's that drawing of a Smurf on your STEM project?" he asks.

"I think they all look pretty good," Mikko says. He squints at the pheasant's back mushroom card. "Hey, you spelled that wrong, though. That's a pheasant's back. F-f-f-f. F-f-f-f. It should start with an *F*."

I fluff his hair up. "That's almost right," I say. "But *PH* makes an *F* sound, too."

He grins up at me, feeling proud. "Come on, Alexi. Let's watch TV," he says. Soon the noise of a cartoon and mindless giggling from the boys fill the living room. One card at a time, I fill up my project board.

Just after six, Toivo pulls up. I dab hot glue on the back of my last card, black currant, and stick it under PLANTS. There. All done. I grab the back of my neck and rub out a kink.

Toivo uses his boot to open the door. His face is hidden behind three large grocery bags. I dash to the door and grab the middle one from him. I try to recall the last time I saw him bring home groceries. I realize I have no memory of it. Once in while he'd stop and pick up a few things, like ketchup or seasoning salt, but he's never, not once, purchased this many at one time.

I set the bag down on the floor and peek in. Crackers, cereal, chips, noodles, rice, canned soups.

"What's all this?" I ask.

He sets his bags down on the counter. Keeping his back to me, he says, "Uh, just some stuff." He reaches down and pulls out grapes, apples, pears, bags of carrots and celery. "Got my first paycheck."

He turns to me. His head hangs low. His eyes hang down, too. I'm not sure what to say.

He turns back around and slowly removes the rest of the groceries. A canned ham. Pickled herring. Milk. Orange juice.

He shuffles his boots but then stands up a little straighter. He fiddles with his hearing aid.

"There won't be much to find out in the woods until spring," I say.

"Right," he says. He opens a jar of mayonnaise. "Want a sandwich?"

"Yeah," I say. "I'm starving."

*   *   *

The boys sit at the table and stare up at my STEM fair project while they eat their sandwiches like gentlemen. Toivo and I stand near the table chewing ours, too. I jab my hand into the potato chip bag he holds and grab a handful.

"Looks good," he says. "Looks very, um, organized."

I crunch a bunch of chips. The salt and the oil taste like a magic concoction.

"Is it boring?" I ask.

"Yes," says Alexi. "It's all black and white. You could at least draw a zebra on it."

"Or a skunk!" adds Mikko. "And a killer whale with a penguin on its back!"

"Shhh," Toivo says to them. "No one asked you, pals. And...it's not boring," he says to me. "I think it's great you thought of all this." He licks his fingertips and shakes the potato chip bag. "I'm only buying these once in a while. They're not good for you."

Mikko and Alexi grab for the bag. "They are good for you. They have potatoes in them."

Toivo holds it up above his head and says, "No way. Finish up. Let's get your reading homework done." The boys jump up and down and try to reach the bag. Toivo crumples it up and tosses it into the garbage. The boys groan and slump their shoulders, but they head-dive onto the couch and then pretend to melt off it. Toivo throws them their backpacks, which they unzip and dig into for their homework.

Upstairs I fill the tub with water, and steam fills the bathroom. Already my muscles ease up. When I get into the water, I lie back and stare up at the ceiling. I close my eyes.

When I open them again, the water has turned cool. I sit up and listen, wondering how much time has passed. It's absolutely silent in the house. Which means one of two things: The boys are sleeping. Or they're up to no good.

When I get down the steps, the first thing I notice is that the garage light is on. Toivo must be out there working on something. The next thing I notice is that my project is missing from the table.

My project is missing.

"Boys!" I shout.

Silence.

I decide then that my tone may have been too sharp and now they might be afraid of me. "Miiii-kkkkkkooooo?" I croon. "Alexiiiiii?"

No response.

The screen door opens. Toivo is wiping grease from his hands onto a dirty rag. "Hey," he says. "I thought I heard someone yelling in here." He scrubs the tips of his fingers with a corner of the towel.

"Yeah." I twist the ends of my hair. "I'm just looking for my project. Did you move it?"

He glances at the table and then leans into the living room. "Where are the boys?" he asks. "They're supposed to be reading their books."

Two picture books lie open on the couch.

We look at each other. Then we take off in different directions to search the house. I skip every other step as I run up to their bedroom. Door's closed. Light's shining from beneath the door. "Toivo!" I shout. Then I turn the knob and fling open the bedroom door.

Turkey feathers fly up and float back down to the floor.

"What in the world—?" I begin.

Toivo appears behind me, looks over my shoulder

into the room, and gasps. He slaps his hand over his mouth. "Oh my God," I can hear him murmur. "I shouldn't have trusted them alone for one minute."

My project lies in the middle of the floor.

The boys sit in front of it, grinning from ear to ear. Mikko has a hammer, and Alexi has the hot-glue gun.

"We're helping," says Mikko.

"It's not boring anymore," says Alexi.

Chapter 22

Rows of card tables fill the gym, wall to wall. Some projects have flashing lights, some have colorful test tubes, some have flowering plants, some have sparkling crystals. All of them look better than mine. I see Alkomso already setting up. And she's getting help from her dad. I can't remember the last time I saw her dad. Every time I went over to their apartment, he was gone working.

The table next to hers and Mark-Richard's is open. I hold my board up over my face and cut between and dodge around the other kids fast. When I get to Alkomso, I say, "Hey."

"Hi!" she says. She's all dressed up. She's even wearing a little bit of lip gloss. If she's still mad at me, she's not acting like it. "Daddy, look," she says. "It's Fern."

"Hi, Mr. Isak."

He fixes a letter on Alkomso's board. Then he turns and says, "Fern! I haven't seen you in a long time. Too long!"

"Yes," I agree. "Too long." To Alkomso, I ask, "Where's Mark-Richard?"

"He said he felt nervous and was going to go throw up in the bathroom."

"That's terrible," I say. Alkomso and Mark-Richard's project includes a toothpick apparatus that looks like a tower. I set my board down and take a good look at theirs.

"What does this do?" I ask.

Alkomso unscrews the top off a superglue tube. "It's just a model." She dabs a dot of glue onto a joint where two toothpicks meet. "That's where the drill goes down into the earth, where they shoot water and chemicals down to break into the shale to release the natural gas."

"Wow. You sound smart." I tilt my head. "Does it cause earthquakes?"

She shrugs. "I don't know. Probably. It depends who you ask. Depends which side they're on." She puts the top back on the superglue.

Against a black board, Alkomso and Mark-Richard have put white letters that spell out HOW FRACK-ING WORKS. The white letters are trimmed with gold glitter. "Your project looks awesome," I say. "Really awesome."

"Thanks." She pulls out a lip gloss and smears it over her lips.

Her dad grimaces. "You don't need that. It's too shiny."

Alkomso rolls her eyes and shakes her head. "Dad, you're so old-fashioned."

He gives her a side hug with one arm and tells her "good luck" and that he'll see her after the judging.

"Bye, Dad. Thanks for all your help." Once he's out of sight, she says, "It's been so great having Dad around all the time. But I hope he loosens up a little." She laughs. "He's even driving my mom a little crazy because he's got the radio on the soccer channel every night."

"I'll bet she's happy to have him around more, though."

"Oh yeah. Definitely. Especially with the baby. Dad likes to hold her."

I think about what the change in jobs has meant for Alkomso's family, how it's put them all back together. I think about how having more money around our house has made everything a bit easier for us, too. That seems like a good thing. Just a little bit, I'm worried I'm on the wrong side.

"Are you going to get set up?" Alkomso asks.

My cheeks get hot. "I guess so."

I set my project on top of the table and take off the black garbage bag Toivo and I put over it to keep it protected.

"You better get a move on," Alkomso says. "The judges are supposed to be coming around as soon as the principal gives the opening address."

I stand up the display board, and I take a deep breath before I open it. I slowly open one side. And then even more slowly open the other.

I stand back. Alkomso comes over and tilts her head to one side as she stares at it. "Ahhh," she says. I wait for something more.

"Um," she says again, squinting now.

I pull on the gray hairs behind my ear.

"That is..." she begins.

My head heats up to a boil.

"Totally amazing!" She shakes my arm and jumps up and down. "You rocked it!"

"I did?" I ask.

Along with my identification cards, Mikko and Alexi glued seeds, nuts, spices, leaves, dried mushrooms, and a hundred turkey feathers all over my display. Lastly, Mikko hammered deer antlers to the top.

She nods her head and reads my display from top to bottom. "I'm amazed that all these plants and stuff are out in the woods."

"You are?"

"Of course!" she says. "No way should a wastewater pond go there. No way. Kloche's can put it somewhere else."

"You think so?"

"Sure."

"There has to be a place that's less damaging to the trees, animals, and plants," I say.

"Has to be," she agrees.

Soon Miss Taft, the principal, pounds on a podium and asks for us to quiet down and pay attention.

"Sixth graders!" she yells. "Eyes up here!"

Binders close and chairs shuffle and coughs stifle.

"Sixth graders, judges, and teachers," she says. "Welcome to the judging of the Colter STEM Fair for Sixth Graders!"

Everyone claps and cheers.

"Every year, our students demonstrate the brightest ideas in science, technology, engineering, and mathematics. Our teachers set aside precious instruction time to aid students in their research and questions. Our parents spend countless hours devoting time to helping their children. We are indeed proud of these students today."

Alkomso and I swap glances and smirks. Just then, Mark-Richard opens the gymnasium doors and walks across the floor to where we are. His new shoes squeak the entire way. He slinks up and stands between us. Alkomso pats him on the back. I mouth *Are you okay?* to him. He nods, but his skin is pale and his eyes are red.

"Judging will begin in five minutes. Each student or pair of students will be questioned for the next two hours by experts in their fields. After the judging is over, the gymnasium will be opened to the rest of the Colter students and families and community members for viewing while the judges tally the results.

Finally, the scores will be tabulated and each project will be awarded a white, green, red, or blue ribbon. One project will be chosen as Grand Champion of the STEM fair and earn a purple ribbon. That project will go on to represent Colter in the regional STEM fair in December. One other project will be chosen as Reserve Champion and will serve as backup to the Grand Champion."

Mark-Richard sways back and forth, as though he's about to faint. I lean over and move his chair, and then I tell him to sit down. He does.

"Put your head between your knees," says Alkomso. "So you don't pass out."

"Additionally," Miss Taft goes on, "the Grand Champion will receive a two-hundred-fifty-dollar prize. The Reserve Champion will receive a one-hundred-dollar prize."

Even I clap now. I wonder if they give the prize money in cash or check. I wonder how you cash a check if you're a kid like me, who doesn't even have a checking account.

"Now," Miss Taft says, "let's begin."

A hush falls over the gym. Miss Taft convenes with the judges. They nod and spread out in all directions.

"Good luck," I say to Alkomso and Mark-Richard.

Mark-Richard lifts his head and says, "Good luck."

"You'll do great," says Alkomso.

Every time a judge comes near, we watch anxiously while pretending not to. When the judge approaches a different kid, I immediately feel relief—which lasts about a millisecond, because I know that I'll be judged soon enough. Then I feel even more anxious than before.

I'm about to excuse myself and go get a drink of water when Alkomso and Mark-Richard are approached by a man who says he's a rural economic developer.

He says, "What a fascinating topic. Tell me all about it." He taps a pencil on his clipboard. I decide to skip the water and listen to Alkomso.

At first she looks like a deer in the headlights. Her body is stiff, and her eyes are big and round. The first questions are softballs, so Alkomso loosens up and answers them easily. I wish I had those words, all those words that flow so easily from her mouth. She sounds like a teacher.

But then the judge asks, "Do you think reliance on fossil fuels is unwise? Do you think it contributes to serious pollution problems?"

"Um," she says. "Well, I don't…" Alkomso fidgets and clears her throat.

I feel sorry for her right now. I want to help, but I can't. I want to know the answer, too.

Mark-Richard perks up. His face is still white and sweaty from being sick, but he stands up and crosses his arms. "Look, sir. I know one thing. I love living in a house that heats up with natural gas. From fracking." He wipes his nose. "You ever have to chop wood to heat your house for the *whooole* winter? You know how much work that is? You know how much soot it creates? How kids like me are sick all the time and can't breathe because of it?"

The judge steps back, looking surprised.

"I'd take fracking over that every day of the week," Mark-Richard says. Alkomso and I lock eyes. She looks stunned, and I'm sure I do, too.

Finally, the man asks them if they have anything to add. Alkomso blurts out, "Fracking may cause earthquakes and contaminated water, so this project warrants more research."

The guy drops open his mouth and smacks it closed again and again, like a dying fish. "Thank you," he finally says.

I stare at my feet and practice in my head what to say when it's my turn. *Hi, I'm Fern, and my project is—*

"Ah-hem," someone says. A tall man with slicked hair stands in front of me. "Tell me about your project." On his shirt is his name, MR. RADAR. Below that is COLTER COMMUNITY COLLEGE. I recognize the name; he's a science teacher at the same school Mom taught at.

"Um..." I forgot how I was even going to introduce myself. "Um." My ears ring. My mouth is dry. I take a deep breath. "My name is Fern, and my project is about food in the forest."

He touches his ear with the eraser of his pencil. "You'll have to speak up," he says. "I don't hear very well anymore."

I nod. "That's okay," I say a little louder. "My dad is deaf in one ear, too."

He chuckles. I start to feel a little better. "Food in the forest, did you say?"

"Yes. For my whole life, my family has foraged in the woods."

"Can you define *forage*?"

I hadn't planned for that question. "*Forage* means, like, looking or searching in the wild for your food, I think."

He nods and writes something down on his clip-board. "Tell me what you've found."

I begin pointing to each category. "Most of the things that we find to eat can be categorized into these four areas. Plants. Roots. Nuts. And mushrooms, which are my favorite."

"Hmm," he says. "Why's that?"

"Um, well...when there's not a lot of meat to eat in the house, mushrooms are good for being filling in the same way that meat is."

"I've never thought of that." He looks over my display board. He pulls a pair of glasses out of his pocket and puts them on to read my cards.

"Yes, sir," I add. "They're very good. They're dense and flavorful. And you even prepare them in the same way you would a lot of meats."

He nods again, and he writes down some more notes on his clipboard. "Interesting. And you found all of this where?"

"In Millner's woods," I say. "Right outside Colter."

"Just past the water tower?"

"Yeah. Pretty much there."

"Okay," he says. "One last question, Fern."

"Yes, sir?"

"Are you related to Johanna?"

All my weight shifts to my heels. I might tip over. "Yes, sir. Johanna was my mother."

"Thought so. You look just like her. Wonderful teacher. We miss her a lot."

I steady up. "Thank you, sir."

"Thank you, Fern," he says. "I learned a lot."

After that, I get interviewed by four more experts. One woman and three men. Each one gets a little easier. The most difficult question I get asked comes last.

"May I inquire what deer antlers have to do with foraging in the woods?" he asks.

I'm sure my cheeks are beet red. And I'm trying to keep my sweaty palms from touching my clothes. I decide to just go with the truth. "Well, sir, my little brothers wanted to help. And while I wasn't looking, they nailed them on there."

He blinks at me several times. Then he laughs his head off.

Finally, the judging is over. We're allowed to roam around and check out one another's projects before the doors are opened to the public.

One kid did his project on paper-airplane aerodynamics. He's got six different shapes of planes. Another did hers on the effect of loud rock-and-roll music on houseplants. All the plants are dead. At least three kids did volcanoes. Lame, just like Mr. Flores said. Another kid has a carburetor torn apart and a diagram of how one works. His looks really good. Some kid did a project on bridge design. Another did his whole project on something called the golden ratio.

Lots of kids have "Which Brand Is Best?"–type projects. Toilet cleaners. Paper towels. Dish detergent. Diapers. Those are all pretty boring, too, except for Michelle Berkner's. Her dad is a dairy farmer, so she tested which laundry soap works best to get out cow manure scent. She has before-and-after washings for everyone to sniff.

One girl has Christmas lights all over her project, "Which Nail Polish Lasts Longest?"

"Cool project," I tell her. She's one of Margot's friends. "Which one lasts longest?"

"I don't know." She shrugs. "My mom did the whole thing."

Next to hers is Emily and Margot's project: "Making Eggs Bounce: The Effect of Acetic Acid on Calcium Carbonite."

"Wow," I say. "Do eggs really bounce?"

"Hi, Fern," says Margot. "They do! Don't they, Emily?"

Emily grabs an egg and drops it on the ground. It bounces. "See?"

"Cool," I say.

The gym doors open and parents, brothers, sisters, aunts, uncles, and neighbors flood in. By the time I get back to my project, there's a crowd gathered around my display. A lady points at my wild-plum card. "Is that right outside Colter?" one lady asks another. "Where Kloche's wants to put that disposal pond?"

"I'm not sure," says the other lady. "I sure hope not. That'd be a shame."

They smile at me, and I'm not sure if they want me to answer their questions. I decide to anyway. "Yes. Most of these foods are found in those woods right outside town."

"Oh my goodness," says the first lady. She puts her hand to her chest. "I'm going to write a letter to the editor. We can't let those woods be cut down."

"You know," her friend says, "my mother used to make black-currant jam when we were kids. Seems to me she used to find the currants out in these same woods."

Alkomso and I are talking when a man in a business suit approaches us. He stands back and first eyes my project and then Alkomso and Mark-Richard's. "Quite a conundrum," he says. "But if you girls can discuss it rationally, then I guess we adults should be able to, too." He leans in closer to Alkomso's miniature drilling model. "Can you tell me how this works?" he asks.

"Sure," she says.

An elderly man gets up close to my face. "Young lady," he says. "My dad was a logger out there years ago when they decided not to cut down that stand of trees, and a man named Millner bought it up. Got a nice duck pond on that land, I think."

"That's right, sir," I say. "Kloche's is trying to pressure the county to annex that land from Mr. Millner."

"That'd be a dang shame," he says. "Don't seem right at all." He pats me on the head. "You keep up the good work. Colter needs rangers like you guarding the trees and plants."

Alkomso's mom and dad come by with Kaltumo. Hamdi moons over Alkomso, hugging and kissing her and telling her what a good job she did. Kaltumo wails the entire time. Alkomso's mom hands the baby to me. I bounce her up and down on my hip until she stops crying and giggles. When she starts crying again, I give her to Mr. Isak. "She only likes her daddy," he says, smiling at the baby.

Mark-Richard's foster parents come, too. They seem really nice. They tell him they are very proud of him, and even though he is stiff, they hug him tight. He even smiles and puts one arm around his foster mother, whose name is Amy.

"You did such a great job!" says Amy. Then she tells him they have a surprise for him.

"Really?" he says. "What?"

They turn around and wave for someone to come over. From behind a bunch of adults, Gary runs up and dives into the arms of Mark-Richard.

"Gary!" Mark-Richard screams. He lifts his brother up, even though the kid is pretty big. "Gary, I missed you so much." Gary twists his arms around Mark-Richard's neck and holds on tight.

I'm too big for this, but I have to look away so that I can compose myself and not cry. Seeing Mark-Richard and Gary together again makes my heart light up like a starry night. The foster parents put their arms around each other, and the foster mom wipes a tear away from her cheek. I turn around to let them have some privacy.

The gym is packed with people. I scan all the heads.

"Fern!" I hear. "Fern! Over here!"

Grandpa, taller than everyone, moves through the people like a knife separating a muskmelon.

Chapter 23

Everyone moves out of his way. He lays his giant hand on my shoulder and takes in my poster. "Look at this! This is marvelous!" He stares at the antlers and cocks his head.

"Thanks, Grandpa." My stomach flops. Why is he here? Is he just going to cause trouble with Toivo again? Is he here to see how I've done? Like another test for Toivo?

He pulls out a pair of glasses from his shirt pocket and puts them on to read my cards.

"Wonderful," he says.

Is my project wonderful enough to prove to him

that I'm doing well in school? Knowing Grandpa, it's not unless I win the prize. And there are a lot of good projects, so I know that I'm not likely to win. Especially since mine has deer antlers on it.

"It was nice of you to come," I say, hoping he takes it as a hint to go away. I look around, hoping Toivo isn't here yet. The last thing I want is the two of them together.

The movement of all the people in the auditorium has created its own kind of wind. The feathers on my project dance around. Grandpa reaches up and catches a floating feather. He slips it in my hair, behind my ear. I touch the feather and giggle. "Mikko and Alexi helped me with my project."

"I could have guessed." He studies my project again. "My, my, my." He chuckles. "You are Johanna's daughter. When she was in sixth grade, she made dyes out of things she found outside and around the house." He takes a hankie out of his back pocket and blows his nose. "She got a blue ribbon!" He emits a laugh that has a cry in it.

I love when he tells me about Mom. I want to know everything I'm missing. Now I don't know if I want him to leave or I want him to stay. I take Grandpa's hand and don't care that his are as sweaty as mine.

"She stained every towel in the house," he says. "But her stepmom didn't care. They had a lot of fun figuring out what colors you could get out of different things." He hoists up his belt buckle. "I'm just real proud of you here." He points to the deer antlers. "Let me guess. Mikko and Alexi's idea?"

Just then Miss Tassel approaches us. I guess practically the whole town is here.

"Hello there, Mr. Greene, so nice to see you again," she croons. She's all dressed up in a pantsuit, but there's a stain of some kind on the lapel.

Grandpa bows his head a little bit. "And you as well, Miss Tassel. What do you think of my granddaughter's project here?"

Miss Tassel gives my project a glance without really looking at any of the details. "It's good," she says. "But not as good as the food this young lady prepares. Yummy. I've been craving those pickled ramps since I left." She pokes me in the arm. "Maybe I can come visit again in the spring? Get some?"

"Sure," I say.

My brothers bust through the crowd, and each grabs one of Grandpa's legs. "Grandpa!"

That means Toivo is here, too. My heart pounds. *Please don't fight. Please, please, please don't fight.*

"Oh, my boys," says Grandpa.

"Did you see how we helped Fern?" Mikko lets go of Grandpa's leg and stares proudly up at his contribution to the project as though it's a hot-air balloon in the sky.

"I put on the feathers so it wasn't boring," Alexi says. "Before I helped, Fern made it really boring with only lots of words."

Grandpa hoists him up and slobbers on him with kisses that Alexi wipes off. Alexi kicks until Grandpa sets him down. "You boys did a fine job of helping," says Grandpa. "When you're big, I'm going to put you in charge of my factories."

"I've got to run," says Miss Tassel. She jabs Grandpa in the chest. "We'll be in touch about that proposal I laid out, right?"

"Yes, ma'am," says Grandpa. "Toivo and I will talk it over. We'll get back to you."

Even though we're all connected and what one does affects everyone else, adults have these secret lives that kids can't get into. In the same way, though, kids have secret lives, too. It's like the plants and the animals in the woods: They all depend on each other, but they all have their own way of living there.

"Big John." Toivo arrives in his work shirt, a cigarette behind his ear.

I move to stand in between them.

"Toivo," says Grandpa. He stares at Toivo's work shirt. He moves his mouth as though he's about to say something more, but Miss Taft raps on the podium.

"Attention, please! Attention! We will now begin the ribbon and prize distribution. Students, please remain at your projects."

I don't move. Toivo puts his hand on one of my shoulders. Grandpa puts his on the other. Each side feels like a cement block.

The judges move seriously throughout the crowd. They check their clipboards and then place ribbons on the boards. White, green, red, and blue. The girl to my left gets a blue ribbon hung on her project, and then the judge walks past me and Alkomso and Mark-Richard to put a red ribbon on the project next to theirs. The judge steps back, checks her clipboard, and moves on.

Finally, a different judge stands before Alkomso,

Mark-Richard, and me. Two ribbons dangle from her fingers. A blue one and a deep purple one. My heart races.

"Oh my God," says Alkomso. "Fern!"

I look at her. I can't smile or say anything. It feels as though I got caught out in the cold and my face is frozen. My ears ring like crazy. Could I have won the purple ribbon? The Grand Champion ribbon? The $250 prize? Grandpa squeezes my shoulder.

The judge checks her clipboard, and then she reads my project title. She hangs a blue ribbon on the corner of my board.

My heart sinks.

Grandpa drops his hand from my shoulder. "What?" he says.

Toivo pulls me into his side. I want to hide behind him. I didn't win.

"You did great," he whispers.

Tears well up in my eyes. Grandpa looks at Toivo and says loudly, "Can you believe that? This is ridiculous. Fern's project is outstanding. My granddaughter—"

"Shhh," Toivo says to him.

Grandpa looks as though he's about to let Toivo have it for shushing him. But then Grandpa looks at me and sighs. His eyes are getting glassy, too.

Miss Taft smacks the podium. "Ladies and gentlemen! Attention, please!"

Everyone quiets.

"Students of Colter Elementary," she says, "congratulations on another successful STEM fair. As your administrators and teachers, we want to extend our pride in your work." She pauses as everyone claps. "And now the moment you've all been waiting for." She shuffles a few papers.

I'm embarrassed because I know my eyes are watery, but I look at Alkomso, who is looking right at me.

"You did great," she whispers.

I can't even smile.

Miss Taft continues. "The Reserve Champion is, for 'How a Carburetor Works,' Matthew Klein."

From one pocket of the gym, a few people hoot and holler. Grandpa crosses his arms and groans.

Miss Taft waits for the crowd to quiet down. Then she continues. "Finally, the Grand Champions, who will represent Colter Elementary School at the regional STEM fair, are Mark-Richard Haala and Alkomso Isak, for 'How Fracking Works.'" The judge steps forward and hands Alkomso the purple ribbon.

The blood drains from my face. Alkomso beat me. Fracking beat the woods.

Alkomso gives the ribbon to Mark-Richard, who stares at it likes it's a golden egg.

Toivo takes his arm off me and claps. When a big tear slips down my cheek, I quickly wipe it away. I am a big loser. Losing in public makes it even worse. I lost in front of my brothers, in front of Toivo, and in front of Grandpa. I wish the earth would swallow me up. Toivo elbows me until I clap, too. Slowly.

Mark-Richard rubs his fingers over the lettering of the ribbon. He looks up at the ceiling and then smiles really big. "I've never won anything before!" he says. Alkomso high-fives him. I clap harder. I clap like I really mean it, until I do really mean it.

When Alkomso's and Mark-Richard's families swarm them and no one is paying attention to me, I reach up and snatch the blue ribbon off my project and stuff it in my pocket. Only Grandpa and Toivo see. I slide in close to Toivo and hang my head, hair falling all around my face like curtains. Toivo puts his arm around me again and pulls me close. His new shirt smells like plastic, but I don't care.

"Fern," Grandpa says. He pulls out his wallet.

"Fern, how about you stay with me tonight?" He slides a bill out and extends it toward me. "You did a great job. You take this and buy yourself something nice with it." It's a $100 bill. "We'll go shopping tomorrow in the big city, how about?"

Toivo squeezes me. My little brothers jump up and try to reach the bill.

"Thanks, Grandpa," I say. "But I think I'd rather go home tonight. I think I'd just rather go home with Toivo and the boys."

Alexi springs up and, with his good arm, snatches the bill from Grandpa. Like hounds playing with a bone, the boys hover over the money, turning it, flipping it, smelling it. Toivo taps my side.

"But maybe tomorrow," I say. "Um. Maybe tomorrow we can come over and watch a movie with you or something?"

"Yeah," says Toivo. "I'd be happy to drive them over for the day. If you want."

Grandpa fiddles with his wallet, finally closing it and putting it back in his pocket

"Big John?" says Toivo.

Grandpa looks up. His cheeks are wet. He nods several times. He reaches into his pocket again. This time, instead of his wallet, he yanks out his hankie. After he blows his nose, he says, "I'd like that." He comes over and kisses my head. "I wasn't sure what to expect tonight. Wasn't sure you were going to pull it off, to tell you the truth."

I'm afraid he's going to mention that I *didn't* actually pull it off.

"But I underestimated you. You did a fine job here." He pinches his nose with his hankie, wipes both nostrils. "I underestimated all of you," he says.

Toivo shuffles his feet. "You don't have to—" he begins.

"Yes," interrupts Grandpa. "Yes, I do. Now, I like that proposal Miss Tassel put together. I can live with that so long as you keep up the work and the kids keep up their schooling."

Toivo nods slowly.

Grandpa hugs me. "Your mom's hair used to smell like that, too." He sighs. "I'll see you tomorrow, I hope?"

Toivo nods. "I think that's going to work out fine."

"Good, good," says Grandpa. "Gives me a chance to see the grandkids, and you a chance to put in some overtime."

After Grandpa leaves, I glance at Toivo. I don't even have to ask. He knows what I want to know.

"Miss Tassel," he begins. "Well, she thought up an arrangement that's pretty agreeable."

"And?"

"She, uh…she, uh, suggested that you kids spend one weekend a month with Big John. Grandpa, I mean. That you spend one weekend a month with Grandpa during the school year and then two weeks with him in the summer." Toivo rubs his chin with his free hand.

"Oh," I say.

"But I was going to ask you first before I agreed."

"You mean I get a say?" I stare at his eyes.

"Yeah. You get a say."

I think about it for a few seconds. "No more letters from Children's Protective Services?" I ask.

"Nope," he says.

"No lawyers or fighting with Gramps?"

"Right. No more."

"Yeah. I can live with that." I tuck my hair behind my ears. "I like that plan."

Chapter 24

When the crowd finally clears out a little, we begin packing up our projects. Alkomso's dad is being extra careful with hers and Mark-Richard's because they've got to take it to the regional STEM fair in a couple of weeks.

Just as I'm about to congratulate them, the judge walks up and hands Alkomso the check.

"Oh my God!" she squeals.

"Alkomso!" her dad scolds. "We don't use that language."

"Oh my *goodness*, I mean." She rolls her eyes again and looks at me like *Dad is such a drag*.

"Let me see it!" I do my best to sound cheerful. I want to be, but I still feel like a failure, so it's hard. Even if Alkomso is my best friend, even though I am proud of her, I still feel really let down. Mostly I feel disappointed in myself. Mostly I wonder if I'm just wrong. I wonder if everyone thinks fracking is more important than my mushrooms, my ramps, and my beechnuts. I wonder if fracking really is more important than the bears, the coyotes, and the wild turkeys. I wonder if I just embarrassed myself in front of the whole school and the whole town for nothing.

"What should we do with it?" Alkomso asks me.

"I don't know. I guess you should celebrate with it."

Alkomso scratches her head. "I don't know.... I've been thinking. What if we, like, I don't know, what if we bought some of those trees or something? So that they can't be cut down?"

I know $250 isn't enough for even one tree, but her words make me feel a little better. "That's nice of you. But I think you should spend it on your family. For a party or something."

A woman with a notebook taps Alkomso on the shoulder. "Excuse me. I'm with the newspaper," she says.

She must be a reporter. I step back to make a little room.

"Hi!" says Alkomso.

"I'm doing a story on the STEM fair for the *Colter Crier*. Are you the winner?"

"Yeah." Alkomso extends her hand for a shake. Then she yells to Mark-Richard, who is standing with his foster family, to get over here. "Well, me and Mark-Richard." Mark-Richard comes over.

"Good, good," the reporter says. "I'm going to want to talk to you. Can you point me to the girl who did the project on 'Foods of the Forest'? I mean, this is just fascinating. Two projects, one from each side of the fracking argument. This is going to be a great story."

Alkomso grabs my arm and yanks me to her. "Here she is. And we're all best friends! All three of us. Will you add that to your story?"

The reporter opens her notebook and writes something down. Without looking up at us, she says, "Names?"

For the next ten minutes, Alkomso, Mark-Richard, and I answer her questions. When she finishes, the reporter says, "Thanks, kids. Maybe you don't know it, but the whole crowd was talking about this issue because of your projects. Half of them want to let

Kloche's go on. Half of them want to save the woods. You've started quite a stir in this small town."

"Mr. Flores, our science teacher, told us to pick something that was important to us and to our town," Alkomso adds.

"Who?" says the reporter. "The teacher who was put on leave by the school board? Him?"

"He's a great teacher," I say.

"It's total bunk that they won't let him teach," says Mark-Richard.

The reporter reopens her notebook and scribbles some more. "This story gets hotter by the second. I'll get in touch with him for a quote. I'm sure he'd be very proud of you."

I hear the gym door open and slam, like it does if you don't know to close it softly.

I stand on my tiptoes to see. I squint.

It's Horace Millner, leaning against the doorframe with his cap low over his eyes. When he sees me, he wags his finger at me to come over.

"I'll talk to you later," I say to Alkomso and Mark-Richard. "Congratulations again."

I pass where my brothers and Gary sit under my project table, staring at the money. I pass Toivo as he's packing up my project. "I'll be right back," I tell him.

He sees Millner. "Take your time."

My heart pounds, afraid that Millner is here to deliver bad news about Ranger or to tell me that he's changed his mind. That it's too much work to fight the frackers. That he's going to sell the woods. I can't think of any reasons for him to be here except for bad ones.

"Hi, Mr. Millner," I say.

"Got to show you something," he says. "Okay with your dad if you come with me out to the lot for a minute?"

I look back at Toivo, who's watching. Millner and Toivo nod at each other.

"Sure," I say. The large gym doors swing open into the evening. The sun is already going down. Most of the cars are gone. Millner's truck sits in the middle of the lot. Sitting next to it is Ranger.

"Ranger!" I dash to the dog.

"Careful!" Millner calls after me. "Careful. He's all broke up inside."

I kneel down a few feet away. Ranger's left side is wrapped up in white cloth. At first, I think that his front leg must be bundled up inside the bandage.

"Ranger." I raise my hand for him to smell. "Remember me?"

Millner approaches, scratches Ranger behind the ear.

A long crimson line stains the wrap from Ranger's chest to his belly. The area there seems caved in. "His leg?"

"Had to come off," says Millner. "Dog was a real trooper. Or Ranger, I guess, if that's what you call him. Never named my dogs."

I creep closer and pet Ranger between the eyes, and he stands it without complaint. Ranger's eyes are dull, like there's no fight behind them. When he breathes, he rasps.

Millner clears his throat. "He's not doing too good, though. Truth is, he's not going to make it. I thought you'd want to..."

Ranger's going to die. Millner brought him to say good-bye. I rest my cheek against Ranger's nose. "You've been a fine friend, Ranger."

From inside the cab of the truck comes a bitty whine. Ranger perks, pants, and raises his nose.

"Brought you something," Millner says, "if it's all right with your dad." He opens up the door and pulls out a box, sets it on the ground. Then he opens the top. A little wet nose, the size of a bean, pokes up and sniffs the air. "My dog had a litter."

A German Shepherd–like pup scratches along the sides of the box to see out. Just like his dad, he's got gray fur around his muzzle.

"This one," Millner says, "looks just like his daddy. I thought you might like him."

I lift him out, tiny thing, weighing about the same as a loaf of oat bread, and cradle him against me. He smells like sour milk and wet straw. Ranger sniffs him, too. And the little pup wags his tail and gets so excited he pees on me.

The gym doors open, and my brothers burst out and gush over the pup's cuteness. They want to hold him. They want to pet him. They want to name him.

Ranger stretches out on the pavement and closes his eyes.

"Forget it, you guys," I say. The little pup climbs up into the nook of my neck. "Partner is his name," I say. "He's my little Partner."

I rub my thumb over his back and imagine him growing up, napping on a rug in my room, running wild through the woods with the boys, sitting at my feet while I do my homework, and being a pal through rich times and lean days.

Toivo comes up, with my project wrapped back up in the garbage bag. He says, "What do we have here?"

"This is our new dog!" says Alexi.

Toivo raises his eyebrows.

"If it's all right with you," says Millner. "I thought Fern might like him."

Toivo nods. He and Millner light cigarettes and talk for a while as the sun goes down on Colter.

I don't know if Kloche's will cut down Millner's woods. I don't know if Toivo's new job will last or if he'll keep it or if we'll always feel poor. I don't know if Ranger will last one more hour or one more day.

Even though I just met him, I know Partner's got Ranger's grit, and I make a promise to Ranger and to his pup to raise Partner right, with mettle.

I stroke him on the ears, and in the sunset, his fur glows silver.

Chapter 25

It's springtime again, and the fiddle-heads are uncurling in Millner's woods. Partner races out ahead of the boys and me. Partner's only as high as my knees, but he thinks he's a big dog. He barks at every bird and butterfly he sees, as though he's the boss of the grove. When we're out walking, his yapping draws the rest of Millner's wild pack of family dogs into the woods. The rest but Ranger, of course.

Ranger died before Christmas. Millner picked at the freezing ground until a deep-enough grave was dug and buried him out here near the pond, where the ducks like to flock in fall. Millner thought Ranger would like that.

"Partner!" Alexi says. "Get back here!" He races after Partner, waving his arms and shouting. Millner's dogs come howling through the trees.

"They're going to trample the mushrooms," says Mikko.

I'm scouring the forest floor. "Oh, let them be," I say. "You were wild like that, too, when you were little." Mikko shakes his head as though he doesn't believe it. He's grown an inch in height but a leap in sense since last fall. He's been easier to mind. He helps with Alexi, who is still wild.

Tonight, after Toivo gets home from work, we're having a little party, a cookout, with Gramps, Mark-Richard's foster family, Alkomso and her family, and Millner. Even Mr. Flores might come if he can get his grading done.

Last fall, after the STEM fair, the *Colter Crier* ran a big article about fracking, Millner's woods, and Mr. Flores. Since then the town has put a moratorium on Kloche's wastewater pond. *Moratorium*, I learned, means "a pause while we think about it." Anyway, enough people supported Mr. Flores that he got his job back.

I have Mom's recipe book. While we can afford to buy more groceries now, there are some ingredients you just can't get at the store. I need morels. I need fiddleheads. I need ramps, and no grocery store stocks those.

Mom named me for fiddleheads, the tight curls of the early fern plant. They are jade green with a slight silver sheen. They rise up out of the dirt about the same time as the morel mushrooms and ramps do.

I stop and kneel down. Sometimes it's best if you get as low as possible. You start to see things in a different way. Mikko trudges on ahead. He stops beneath a dead ash tree and turns back to me. He gives me a thumbs-up. That means he's found the morels. Soon he's bent over, picking them and tucking them into his sack.

I push aside some of last autumn's dead leaves. Sticks and dirt underneath. I can smell them. Fiddleheads have a fish odor. I know they're here. I carefully scrape away more dead leaves. They're wet and soggy, and I begin to wonder if I'm mistaking that smell for fern babies, until my fingers feel new growth.

Duck Breasts and Fiddleheads

Get somebody else to grill the duck on the grill to rare. Duck is so fussy. Never been able to do it. In the meanwhile, heat the saucepan with olive oil or butter. Toss in the sliced morels (make sure you've rinsed them in a salt bath first to chase out all the slimy and buggy critters) and fiddleheads. Fry for three or four minutes. Toss in the ramps for another minute. Done. Lay aside the grilled duck on a nice white plate. A dinner for those in heaven.

Carefully plucking away the old maple, oak, and ash leaves and tossing them aside, I see them: little grayish-green sprouts coiled up like small galaxies. I pinch one off and pop it in my mouth. It's an explosion of fresh wildness.

Author's Note

A few years ago, despite an organized effort to protect it, a prairie near my house in southern Minnesota was partially excavated for frac-sand (silica-sand) mining. While silica sand had been mined here for years, the boom of hydraulic fracturing (fracking) in North Dakota and Texas and elsewhere dramatically increased demand for this type of sand. During the fracking process, silica sand, along with water and chemicals, are forcefully injected into the earth to fracture bedrock and prop open the fissures. Oil and gas are then released and captured.

What convinced many people here to accept the overseas company's operation were the promise of jobs and the proposition that when the mining was over, the company would restore the environment to the best of its ability. Smart people made reasonable arguments on both sides. But the ecological cost from the loss of animal and plant habitat throughout the duration of the mining is striking.

The long grasses where foxes, coyotes, turkeys, pheasants, and deer used to roam are gone, replaced by a deep, open pit with trucks and cranes and noise, surrounded by fences and signs warning trespassers to stay out.

And surrounded by a lot of mystery, too. How many jobs, exactly, did the operation create, for instance? Do the jobs pay a living wage? Is silica-sand mining safe? Is the fracking that the sand is used for safe? Is fracking really a bridge from fossil fuels to renewable energy sources? What are the unintended consequences?

Like Fern, my main character in this story, I'm a nosy person. I wanted answers to all those questions. But the answers, at this moment, depend upon whom you ask. Initially, before the prairie was cleared, the answers from the company and the policy makers seemed vague but positive: *A lot of jobs. Good-paying jobs. We don't know of any long-term environmental consequences.* Many people, desperate for improved economic situations for their families and towns, took them at their word.

But "a lot of jobs" is a relative measurement. "Good-paying jobs" to communities with nearly 30 percent of people living in poverty is also a qualified response. Is mining safer for workers than logging, agriculture, and construction, where more people are maimed or killed every year than in any other occupation? Yes. But is that a good enough reason to keep doing it? Is fracking a cleaner source of energy than, say, coal? Maybe. But some might argue that it's not even possible to predict the long-term environmental impacts of large-scale fracking because we haven't seen it at this scale before. Is fracking a "bridge" to cleaner energy? To some, it is. To others, it is simply another way for companies owned by wealthy people to further exploit natural resources and desperate communities. And to others still, both of those things are true at the same time.

As I visited our local mining site and talked to my neighbors who were also directly affected by the operation, the inspiration for this story was born. I placed my characters in a rural community in Michigan, rich in natural resources but embattled with poverty. Rural poverty is real. Rural food deserts are real. Rural joblessness is real. The struggles of Fern's family are ones I see often, which is why there's sometimes a rush to embrace any new industry promising employment, even when it is temporary, even when the downside is environmental destruction. The economics of the home usually come before people's public positions on energy, environment, and climate change.

For Fern's family, the presence of a fracking site has an immediate impact on her family because it threatens to clear an area she relies upon for food to make room for a wastewater pond. For her family, foraging is a necessity, not a precious or quaint hobby. For my family, foraging is a fun activity. While you should never, ever eat anything from the wild unless you and an informed adult have done enough research to make absolutely certain what you find is safe and won't make you sick, exploring the natural world and learning about the bounty of edibles out there is something I wish American children experienced more.

I'm deeply concerned by how profit-seeking businesses can distance us from understanding how the natural world works, or worse, destroy it completely. A close connection to the plants, animals, bugs, soil, and water helps us appreciate our role on the planet and be more respectful of it. You cannot spend a day in the woods or at the river without being deeply humbled by the awesomeness of nature. And you cannot spend a day in the wild without becoming just a little bit smarter than you were before. The original teacher is out there.

We must bring our children back to the trees. We must get right with our environment. We can't make informed decisions about food, water, or energy from a position of ignorance.

Too many people insist upon pitting economy and environment against each other, as though each being healthy at the same time is not possible. I disagree. We can do better. We just have to want to.

To learn more, I recommend these websites:

Natural Gas Extraction/Hydraulic Fracturing, US Environmental Protection Agency
https://www.epa.gov/hydraulicfracturing

Department of Environmental Quality, Michigan
http://www.michigan.gov/deq/

Midwest Forage Association
http://midwestforage.org

Acknowledgments

Thanks to Faye Bender, Andrea Spooner, Deirdre Jones, and all the wonderful people at Little, Brown and Company. Thanks to Mark Richard for "Strays." And, most heartfully, thanks to Isabella, Mitchell, Phillip, Violette, Archibald, Gordon, and Erik Koskinen, my real-life wild family pack.

Read on for an excerpt from

Wonder at the Edge of the World

by Nicole Helget

✦ CHAPTER 1 ✦

On days such as today, when the wind blows over the flat Kansan plain, I like to amble out to the slow slope of the clover hills and wheat acres to explore and to think.

"Keep an eye on Mother," I say to my sister, Priss.

Mother lifts her head as though she's about to say something. Priss and I both wait and hold our breath, but Mother closes her eyes, rocks in her chair, and returns to her muted world. Priss sighs. She favors our mother, who used to be known as the Beauty of New Bedford, in looks, delicate and fair. I favor Father.

"Make sure she eats something today," I add. Even though Priss is older and more responsible in some ways, I like to tell her what to do every now and then. Surely she doesn't need me to give her anything more to do, though. Priss does all the cooking and the mending, and the cleaning and laundry, too.

"Stay out of town," Priss says. She wrings out an old rag in a bowl of water mixed with vinegar and lemon. She's trying to wipe the soot off the windows, but all she's doing is leaving smears. It's not her fault. Ash from the fires in Tolerone floats on the air always, even though our farm is a couple of miles from town. It settles on the windows. It creeps up beneath the cracks between the floorboards and doors. There's a skim of ash on the surface of the water in our drinking barrel. There's ash on the blade of the bread knife. We drink ash. We eat ash.

I pull the hairpins out of my bun, put them in my mouth, and finger the snarls out of my hair. Ash from my scalp gets under my nails. It's a constant reminder of the tempers in town and in the whole territory of Kansas between the abolitionists and the slave owners.

Earlier this week, an abolitionist set fire to Carson's

livery because Carson's a slave owner. And last week, a slave owner set fire to the schoolhouse because the teacher is an abolitionist. It's summertime, so no one was there and no one got hurt, thank goodness.

Anyway, I don't care if Tolerone ever rebuilds that school. I never learned a thing there. Since Father's been gone, I learn everything on my own, and that's the way I like it. Priss, on the other hand, thinks rebuilding the school is very important. She has designs on being a teacher, I think. As prim and proper as she is, she'd probably make a wonderful teacher.

"Hallelujah Wonder!" Priss says. "Are you listening to me? Stay away from Tolerone."

"I heard you the first time," I say, still holding the pins in my mouth. I try to twist my mop back into a proper bun at the nape of my neck.

Priss wipes the window again. She won't stop until she hears a squeaking sound. "It's dangerous in town with everybody fighting all the time," she says. A squeak. She turns to face me and raises her eyebrows, which means she's serious. "It's *dangerous.*"

"I know that," I snap. I don't like her telling me what to do so much, but she can't help that, either. She thinks she's responsible for me because she's older. I tell her all the time that I can take care of myself. I wasn't planning on going into Tolerone in the first place. In the second place, it's none of her business if I *was* planning on going into town.

"All right, then," Priss says. Her eyebrows drop, and she smiles a little bit. "Let me help you." She puts the rag in the bowl and comes to me. She pulls the hairpins from my mouth. With a yank, a turn, and a tuck, she tames my hair into a bun. Then she spins me around to take a look at her handiwork. "Now, that's better," she says. "Go. Enjoy yourself."

Everyone has always said that Priss will make a fine wife and mother someday. To my knowledge, no one has ever said either of those things about me. Lots of ladies in Tolerone are trying to get Priss, who's fifteen, to marry one of their kin. One noteworthy thing about Kansas is that there are two men for every woman.

Before I go, I straighten the blanket over Mother's feet, which are always cold. Mother remains thin-lipped, and she exhales. I know she's thinking about our old home and old life in Massachusetts. I know she's imagining salty air, seagulls, and fish stews. In her gray eyes, I can sometimes see the bay where we used to live. "Poor Mother," I say. She isn't well. She's not sick, though. She's heartbroken, which is just as awful.

Mother rarely says a word. Most of the time, I feel sorry for her. But sometimes, though I don't mean to, I get angry with her for sitting in a chair quiet as the grave. I want her to stand up and talk and do the work that Priss does. Sometimes I want her to be a mother again. When she can't, or won't, I have to get away from her. Once in a while, I'm afraid that if I don't, I might shout at her. Today is one of those days.

I walk outside into the beige-white light of the sun.

"Be back for supper!" Priss calls after me. "And put on your bonnet!"

I don't answer, and I don't put on my bonnet, either. Priss says the sun is the reason my face is so red and why I've got freckles all over my nose and cheeks, but I don't mind. I raise my face to it instead. The smoke has made the big skies strange with colors, like pinks and purples.

I walk for a while. My skirt hem brushes against forbs and shrubs, most blooming with tiny flowers. Wherever I go, bees and grasshoppers scatter. I choose a spot and sit to listen to my own breathing for a bit. In. Out. Whoosh high. Whoosh low. I inhale the hot, dry air. I exhale the hot, dry air.

From somewhere across the plain, a voice seems to be calling to me. It's like that sometimes out here. Ghost calls float on the never-ending wind. More than one Kansas housewife has gone batty chasing the calls of specters. One lady got so lonesome that she started talking to her chickens as though they were people.

I'd never do something silly like that. Not me. I know ghosts aren't real. There's no scientific evidence that supports the existence of ghosts. Still, I think I hear it, a strange call I know I can't be hearing. So I tell my brain to think about something else. One thing I don't want to be is a senseless Kansas lunatic. That wouldn't be very scientific at all.

For a time, I study the ground, until my eyes adjust to the workings of the tiny world of ants. Once I spot one, it's suddenly easy to see them everywhere, scurrying in their efforts to carry grains of dirt out of their burrows to make room for eggs and food.

If it's a new type of ant that I've never before seen, I'll very carefully disable a live one (meaning squish it firmly and then stick it onto a paper) so I can study it again later. Today, all these ants look the same. Instead of ants, I pick up rocks and look underneath them for sow bugs or grubs or worms. I check the rocks for specks of gold or ribbons of copper or maybe even fossils. But there's nothing new to find.

Finally, I lie down in the grass. For a while, I think about Massachusetts, where life was a lot better. I hold my breath until a noise like the swooshing of water fills my ears. Soon I can almost feel the earth rocking beneath me. I pretend I'm on a ship and the sea is dipping and bobbing. If I squint, the thin streaming clouds against the sky are the sails that guide a ship. On the windward side, the waving wheat glistens like gentle waves. On the leeward side, the curve of a rocky limestone outcropping is the breaching of a sperm whale, coming up for air.

I go on this way for as long as I can, trying to beat however long I held my breath yesterday. Eventually, though, I have to breathe again. And with the oxygen filling my lungs comes back reality, comes back Bleeding Kansas, comes back Father, dead and gone, and comes back the great responsibility I have of carrying on the Wonder name.

✦ CHAPTER 2 ✦

One thing you should know about me is that even though my name is Hallelujah, I like to be called Lu. I can hold my breath longer than anyone I know, a full two minutes. And you should know that even though I'm a girl, I'm smart, or as Father used to say, "Lu, you've got a good knot in your skull."

I'm going to be a scientist. As far as I know, that'll make me among the first lady scientists in the whole world, and certainly the first lady scientist in Kansas—maybe the only scientist at all in this sunbaked, thorny-plant, tree-lonely, dirty-water, skinny-animal, dusty-air, grasshopper-happy, God-forsaken place. Have you ever been to Kansas? I wouldn't come if I were you. For one, it's dangerous. For two, there's nothing to do here.

When I'm a scientist, I will sign on with an oceanic expedition and travel to the far reaches of the earth, just like Father did. I'll call myself an oceanist, a person who studies everything in the ocean, from the currents to the largest whales. On my expedition I'll discover new species of birds, fish, and plants. I'll sketch their likenesses and write careful entries in a journal about their behaviors and dwellings. I'll take samples of these specimens and preserve them. That way, people everywhere will be able to enjoy them and imagine what life is like somewhere else, which is a thing everyone is wont to do at least once in a while. I know I do all the time.

One nice thing about Kansas is that it's so boring that nothing is likely to interrupt you when you are imagining about living somewhere else. Lots of times, I just sit and imagine for hours and hours. I imagine what life would be like if our family had stayed in New Bedford, Massachusetts, the most beautiful and interesting city in America. It is the city where Father was born and Mother was born and Priss was born and I was born. Since staying there wasn't possible, sometimes I imagine what life would be like if we had stolen a boat and sailed away from America rather than come here to Tolerone, Kansas, where nothing remarkable or scientific ever happens, except for a cyclone once in a while. I've never seen one yet, even though the folks here talk about them as if they happen all the time. If I did see one, I'd probably run right into it and hope it would fly me away from here. Until then, I guess I'll just have to make do with my imagination.

I imagine what life might be like among the island peoples or the African tribes or in the Orient or the Mediterranean. Sometimes any place in the world seems like it would be better than Kansas. Probably even Antarctica is better, though only whales, seals, and penguins live there. I'm sure it's a very interesting and scientific place, even if no one really knows much about it. One day I'll see that frozen continent. When I'm a scientist, I'll study the hunting behaviors of killer whales and document the migratory routes of sperm whales. I'll feel the spray of their spouts and fluke splashes on my cheek if I have to follow them all the way to Antarctica.

Do you know anyone who has seen Antarctica? I bet not. Well, it was my father who first discovered it, before the British, the French, and everybody else in the seafaring world out looking for it, as though it were lost. My father explained to me that Antarctica is buttressed by an iceberg fortress and barbed with frigid gales and nearly impossible to penetrate.

But my father did it. He was like that. Persistent and brave and strong. And I am, too.

I have to be because I have a secret. I know the whereabouts of a treasured item. My father trusted me to take care of it, and I intend to be persistent and brave and strong enough to do him proud.

Nicole Helget

is the acclaimed author of the middle grade novels *Wonder at the Edge of the World* and *The End of the Wild*, as well as three adult novels, *The Turtle Catcher*, *The Summer of Ordinary Ways*, and *Stillwater*. She has also coauthored a middle grade novel, *Horse Camp*. She lives in St. Peter, Minnesota, and she invites you to visit her online at nicolehelget.blogspot.com and @NicoleHelget.